THE CHASE

By

Mark T. Sneed

ISBN: 978-1-7366698-3-9

DEDICATION

To my mother, family and friends who continue to inspire, encourage and challenge me to be a better person.

THANK YOU

To all the unsung dreamers, visionaries, believers, questioners, who possess the faith and belief in their convictions despite what others try to say or attempt to shout down what is impossible. Thank you for dreaming not to spite but to enlighten those of what a different perspective and world there is out there and what might be possible.

CONTENTS

Chapter 1. Underwood

For fifty-three days, a little less than three months, instead of walking three blocks from Saint Paul Catholic School to his apartment on Sixth Street Lay walked fifteen blocks west with his cousins to their house on Twentieth. At eleven years old, he had already been a latchkey kid for nearly three years and did not like the loss of his independence. His loss of independence did not seem to matter. His mother had decided it was best for Lay and that was final.

The arrangement was one Lay did not appreciate, at first. In his eleven-year-old mind it just didn't make sense to walk fifteen blocks in the opposite direction of his quiet and comfy apartment which was only three blocks from school. His mother had calmly explained it wasn't safe for a soon to be twelve-year-old to be home alone, especially since their apartment had been broken into on Sixth Street and he had nearly walked in on the robbers.

After the first week Lay sat down in their small apartment kitchen, and at the table and had a short conversation with his mother.

"It's so far," Lay said to his mother who was at the stove warming up some food.

"It's the only solution, for right now," his mother, her egg-shaped face, the color of milk chocolate and with her distinct high cheekbones which made her look like a Native American. "Hanna is going to take care of you until I get off and pick you up." She paused. "It's not forever."

"I don't think they like me that much," Lay said uncertain.

"They love you," his mother said, with a smile from the stove.

Lay pouted. His mother, seeing her son pouting smiled gently and crossed to the table to stroke his cheek. The smile, the touch, the realization his mother was not angry, stunned Lay.

"You're my only son," his mother said, her eyes suddenly brimming with tears. She spun and returned to the stove. "I know you are getting to be a big boy, but you could have been hurt. I don't know what I would have done if those bastards had hurt you."

Lay listened.

A few moments later she returned to the table and sat beside Lay. Her face was wide and freckled with a delicate spray of freckles across her cheeks and the bridge of her nose. Behind wireless round glasses her almond shaped eyes blinked back her emotions. She smiled, her gentle and loving smile and Lay melted. He accepted his fate.

"It's only temporary," his mother said, and Lay had given in. He never complained again.

So, from the second week of April until the end of the school year Lay went to the rear of the Saint Paul Catholic School and gathered with the other kids heading to the other side of the township.

When the school bell rang, Lay would head to the rear of the school, slipping his black backpack on and pushing through the sea of faces going every which way after school. Lay's classroom was close to the rear of the school. His battle to get to the rear was never more than a handful of minutes. When he arrived, he stood around and waited for his older cousin, Hanna, and the other girls to lead them to Twentieth.

It was always his cousins, Hanna and Jordan and about fifteen others, who lived along the way, who walked to the far end of Underwood township. When Hanna and her black and red backpack appeared and the last of her girlfriends showed up at the back of the school they wordlessly signaled, and everyone took off toward Oak Street. The girls, led by Hanna, marched and laughed and talked about school.

The knot of kids as young as seven and as old as twelve followed the most popular girls at Saint Paul's. As they began their march toward the westside of the township some said goodbye to friends heading in the opposite direction. The majority followed Hanna and her handful of influential girls like baby ducklings. The string of younger kids wearing backpacks half their size were somehow related to the girls. They laughed and talked and pushed and played with one another as they fell in step.

Lay, the lone outsider, always found himself in the rear of the group. He walked and noted all the things he never saw the day before. The leaves were turning green, and the grass was growing. Butterflies were flitting around the lawns of houses. Squirrels scurried across the street away from the child parade.

"Keep up, Lathan Alexander," Hanna said as she and her girlfriends marched toward Twentieth.

Hanna was three years older and in eighth grade the year Lay was about to turn twelve. She was preparing for high school. Hanna was a dark brown beauty with big eyes, apple cheeks, full lips and a mouthful of teeth. She was pretty and pear shaped with her hair usually in two gigantic black braids which she either pinned up or allowed to fall to her shoulder blades.

The route to Twentieth was separated by two four lane avenues. The first challenge was five blocks from Saint Paul Catholic School. Ninth Avenue was a busy street as it connected Underwood with Lakewood to the north and Greenwood to the south. Many cars raced down the streets knowing kids had been released from school.

At Ninth Avenue Hanna never crossed without Jordan. She stopped and looked for her baby brother. Jordan was a round faced, brown, good-natured kid who preferred to play than listen to anything. He seemed uninterested in anything but being in everyone's business. Jordan in his mindless, silly and sometime nonsensical way was the exact opposite of the incredibly responsible Hanna. Jordan was goofy and unimaginably carefree. At eight, he didn't seem to have a care in the world other than laughing and being happy.

Hanna always found Jordan before the avenues and personally made sure he got across the street safely. Jordan was three years younger than Lay and in third grade. He was also Hanna's younger brother.

The goofiness and silliness of Jordan disappeared when Hanna spoke. Lay could not help but appreciate Hanna's power. With her call Jordan snapped to attention and ran to his sister's side. He reached out for his sister's hand before crossing the four-lane avenue.

Lay hated the avenues. The drivers seemed to be playing chicken with the school children. They sped up as opposed to slowing down, seeing them crossing. The drivers always appeared angry and agitated if slowing or stopping to allow kids to cross the four lanes was an incredible inconvenience.

The bigger girls gathered the younger kids in manageable groups and ran across the wide street when the traffic ebbed. Lay usually found himself in the last group of kids, the stragglers, and crossed when they did. He was not slow but did not rush to cross the avenues. He crossed the avenues reluctantly always aware of speeding cars.

In small knots of children, they stepped off the curb. They did not pause or hesitate. They ran. Supervised by the girls the younger kids made their way across Ninth Avenue.

It seemed like the drivers thought it amusing to drive faster when kids were on the corners trying to cross. There were close calls every day. Thankfully, no one was hit or injured crossing the avenues.

After Ninth Avenue half of Hanna's friends and ducklings peeled off and headed to their homes and apartments on that side of the Avenue. In the area back toward the east there were still white faces driving around. Saint Paul's sat in the middle of a slowly economic and social shifting neighborhood. The big houses around the church and school were the homes of families that had moved there before the great Northern migration and were loath to move as the township integrated. Maybe thirty or forty homes out of the hundreds of divided and cut up big homes and apartments between Fifth and Ninth Avenue were original owners now.

Lay concentrated on the slow departures of girls who were heading to high school next year. Hanna's friends all. They were heading either to Township West or Sacred Heart an all-girls school in Westwood. Township was where most In Underwood went. It was a gigantic school that housed over two thousand students and by sheer number spit out incredible athletes. Sacred Heart only had four hundred students on its private parochial campus and boasted a ninety-nine percent college acceptance rate. Hanna was heading to Sacred Heart.

All the older girls gave each other hugs as they separated and took their charges home. No girl left without saying bye to Hanna. Everyone loved Hanna.

Seven blocks later it was usually just Hanna, Deanna, Penny, Jordan and a couple of little girls Lay did not know. Deanna, that school year, was wearing a waterproof white backpack. She was a thin shouldered, dark haired girl who had her hair constantly in two loose buns of curly black twists on either side of her heart-shaped face, gold hoop earrings hung on her earlobes. She had arched eyebrows, big, round brown eyes, a straight nose and full lips. Dressed in a blouse, jeans and saddle shoes, Hanna's close friend, lived on Seventeenth and Oak and the handful of remaining kids kept walking up Seventeenth homeward. Lay and Jordan lingered.

A little girl who stood next to Jordan and Lay looked a little bit like Deanna. She had the same hair and big, round brown eyes and straight nose. She was wearing a blue blouse and dark blue knee length shorts. On her feet were a pair of dark blue sneakers.

"You, her sister?" Asked Lay, curious.

The little girl looked at Lay and rolled her big, brown doe eyes as an answer. The little nameless girl with the Afro puffs crossed her arms in front of her small chest and threw out her hip. Lay shook his head at the little girl's attitude. Jordan laughed.

The two girls hugged and acted like they would never see each other again. Every day Lay expected tears, but he never saw any fall.

"You know you're going to see each other tomorrow," Jordan said catching up and walking past the trio.

Deanna hugged Hanna. Penny, the prettier of the three, was the color of honey with square features, dark eyes, a big mouth, full lips and a single dimple on her left cheek. She was shorter than Hanna and Deanna, but more proportional than Hanna. Her arms and legs were equal in length. The muscles in her arms flexed anytime she laughed. Penny looked like she was a female Rock 'Em Sock robot to Lay.

Yet, it was her light dusting of freckles on her cheeks which always reminded Lay of his mother. Penny was pretty, but not flashy. She liked to comb her curly reddish-brown hair in a way that swept it back on one side of her face and on the other allowed her loose curls to play across her small forehead just above her greenish eyes. She was Deanna's close friend as well and on Seventeenth Penny gave her a hug as well.

Lay and Jordan never stopped for the dramatic send offs. They just walked on knowing Hanna and Penny would catch up. Usually, when they reached Nineteenth Avenue, the last four lanes to cross, it was just Hanna and Penny and Jordan and Lay. Hanna would reach out her hand and Jordan would grab it as they prepared to cross.

Penny, the girl with the yellow backpack, would reach out her warm and soft hand and Lay would grab it to just feel the eighth grader's strength and warmth. If she offered to hold his hand Lay wasn't going to miss the opportunity to be pulled along by someone even prettier than Hanna.

Crossing Nineteenth Avenue put the quartet just two blocks from Woodlawn Township. Lay liked Woodlawn Township for the park where he and Jay, his older cousin, hung out and sometimes played basketball.

The four walked on Oak Street and turned left down Twentieth and toward Randolph. Hanna and Jordan lived in the middle of the two hundred block of Twentieth. Penny lived on the five hundred block on

Twentieth on the other side of Washington Boulevard three blocks up the street.

The two close friends hugged and said goodbye while Jordan and Lay just walked to the porch and stood around awkwardly, waiting for Hanna to unlock the front door.

"You know you guys do this every day?"

Hanna ignored Jordan. She and Penny hugged and Lay watched again for tears. None fell. Penny said goodbye to Jordan and Lay and Lay waved goodbye. Jordan ignored Penny usually. Penny walked away and Hanna walked to the porch.

She unlocked the front door of their house and Jordan was always the first to push into the quiet home. Hanna ushered Lay in. Once inside, Hanna pretended to be everyone's mother. Jordan was camped in the living room and watching TV. His backpack would be in the middle of the room, thrown recklessly as he found the couch and the remote.

Lay slipped off one of the backpack straps but did not take off his backpack. He knew the routine. As soon as Hanna had closed the front door Hanna transformed into a drill sergeant. She had work for Jordan to do. In the house, Hanna was boss. No one could just relax. Backpacks were to be put in just the right place. Jordan wanted to go downstairs to his room, away from his sister.

"Turn off the TV. Go do your homework."

With those words Jordan would head downstairs.

"If you stay downstairs, make sure you do your homework. You know I have to check it. So, make sure you do your homework," Hanna said in her best mother voice.

Turning her attention to Lay he could only smile and shake his head. Having heard the same request everyday Lay always smiled when Hanna looked his way. He wanted to ask her why she worried about him? He had good grades. He was never in trouble.

"Lathan Payton Alexander," Hanna began, looking at her younger cousin. "Do you have homework to do?"

"I did it at school," Lay said with a twinkle in his eye.

"Show it to me," Hanna said unimpressed.

Lay would fish out his homework and show the completed work to his cousin.

"Let me see what you're supposed to do this week," Hanna said looking down her nose at Lay.

Lay complied.

"This is due tomorrow?"

Lay nodded.

Hanna never believed Lay. Hanna emptied her backpack on the kitchen table and sorted her textbooks and notebooks, preparing to do her homework. She would look at him with her big eyes and pause, thinking.

"So, what are you going to do until your mom shows up?"

"I could go out back and shoot baskets," Lay said unsure.

"No, that won't work," Hanna said thinking. "Jordan is downstairs and needs to be doing his homework. You dribbling that basketball will get him all distracted."

Lay looked at the TV and shook his head. He looked at Hanna.

"I can sit on the porch and read," Lay said and before Hanna could come up with an alternative he headed to the front of the house and to the living room. He opened the door and sat outside on the porch steps reading anything to wile away the time until his aunt or mom showed up.

When Jay showed up walking from the store it meant Lay had another hour before his mother came to pick him up. In those fleeting minutes before he was picked up Lay loved listening to his older cousin. He seemed so mature.

The other Beck children shrank in Lay's attention when Jay was around. Jay was the oldest of the three Beck children. He was a street-smart kid who seemed so worldly his junior year in high school. He wasn't an athlete. He wasn't particularly great at academics. Jay was sixteen years old and working to get his very own car.

Jay went to the Underwood's predominately black high school, Township West. Lay secretly wanted to go to Township as well but knew that decision was so many years away that it didn't matter.

His cousin worked at the grocery store near Township West as a bagger for a couple of hours a day and on the weekend. The high school was just a bus ride from the Beck home.

When Jay came home from the grocery store, Lay would stop his work, whatever it was, and follow Jay into the house.

"How you doing little man?"

"Good, Jay," Lay would answer with a smile.

He would follow Jay into the house and sit in the kitchen and listen to his cousin and aunt talk about their days. Lay liked listening to the endless stories of his aunt and Jay and Hanna. They always had something important to say.

His aunt Bree worked at a warehouse in the mornings and was usually home an hour after Hanna and Jordan arrived. She had been working at the warehouse for a few years. The warehouse made wires for everything imaginable. His aunt was a supervisor of some line, but Lay was not too sure of the details. Jay was always telling his mother about the grocery store and the politics of the store. Hanna, preparing for high school, was already filling out all her paperwork for the all-girls school she received a scholarship to attend. When her mother arrived at home Hanna always had questions for her mother.

Lay loved to watch as Jay and Hanna battled for their mother's attention. Each story seemed more important than the other and required her full attention on each individually.

Lay secretly loved the fact when he was with his mother it was just her and him. His stories were always given her full attention.

The car horn would sound, and Lay would be in motion. Lay would say his goodbyes to Hanna, Jordan, Jay and his aunt and sometimes his uncle. He would grab his backpack and run out the front door and onto the porch and down the green wooden steps to walkway and to his mother's waiting Volkswagen Beetle. He loved seeing the orange car waiting with his mother behind the wheel.

Lay, just eleven, was still forced to sit in the backseat of the car for his safety. He didn't care. All he cared about was being close to his mother.

Anytime Lay climbed into his mother's car she was playing something on the radio. It didn't matter what, but the Beetle was rarely quiet when his mother drove. His mother drove the Volkswagen like a racecar driver. She had a manual transmission and Lay loved watching his mother pressing the gas, brake and clutch while shifting the stick shift.

"Did you do your homework?"

His mother would be changing gears and turning the steering wheel like Lay had seen professional racecar drivers do on TV. She was always so focused when driving.

"Yes," Lay said with a grin, thinking of Hanna.

"Did you eat?"

"Yes," Lay said as Underwood flitted by. His mother would turn onto Saint Charles, the fastest way home. There were three lights on Saint Charles, Lay knew. His mother was always trying to time the lights, so she didn't have to stop all the way home. It was her thing.

That was Lay's school schedule at the end of his fifth-grade year at Saint Paul Catholic School. It was also the most time he ever spent with Hanna and Jordan and Jay on Twentieth Street.

Chapter 2. Sixth Street

Once home, on Sixth Street, the pair fast walked to the front of the dimly lit apartment complex and its twelve apartments separated by three doors, standing next to each other. At night the apartment complex looked eerie to Lay. His mother pushed Lay inside of the first door to the small lobby of their apartment building. Lay once inside would walk downstairs to their basement apartment as his mother checked the mailbox. In the dimness of the basement landing Lay unlocked and entered the apartment.

Behind the basement door, was a living room overrun by houseplants that seemed to be trying to take over the apartment. His mother had an incredible green thumb. She loved tropical houseplants. In the living room, closest to the windows stood several houseplants as tall as the ceiling. There were a handful of plants which bent at the ceiling and were seeking space above Lay and his mother's head.

The living room was more a jungle than living room. His mother had a sofa and matching chairs there but Lay rarely sat on the couch. It seemed as if the houseplants were watching him any time, he was in the room alone with them. The big stereo and record player were in the living room, but Lay did not go in the living room unless he had to leave the apartment.

It was his responsibility to turn on the lights in the apartment, while his mother waited outside. Lay brushed past the familiar houseplants which dominated the living room. Along the wall which separated the living room from the kitchen sat the color TV. Just a few feet from the TV, on the other side of the living room wall was the small kitchen and kitchen table where Lay and his mother usually sat and ate. By the time Lay had turned on the kitchen lights his mother entered the apartment and locked the front door.

Lay walked through the apartment and turned on the light in the bathroom he and his mother shared. From there he turned on the light in his mother's bedroom and finally his light in his bedroom.

His mother would be in the kitchen when Lay walked back down the hall and to the kitchen.

"You hungry?"

Lay usually was not hungry if he ate over his cousin's house. His mother would usually have the phone cradled against her ear and shoulder as she hastily made something to eat for herself and sometimes Lay. Lay would watch his mother preparing something as she talked on the phone at the same time.

The pair spent most of their time in the kitchen. The small kitchen with oven, sink and refrigerator. In the corner of the kitchen, closest to the living room and hallway to the bedrooms sat the small kitchen table where Lay sat to eat or do his homework or pretend to do his homework while his mother was on the phone. The yellow wall phone with the extra-long cord which could reach all the way to the bathroom was probably the most essential kitchen utility to his mother. She was always on the phone once she was home.

When hungry, Lay would sit and eavesdrop on his mother's conversation with someone he knew. Lay would sit at the kitchen table and try and figure out who his mother was talking to based on the conversation. It was a brain teaser because his mother rarely said anyone's name. Many times, Lay surprised himself at how accurate he was in his guesses.

Not hungry, Lay would watch his mother talking, cooking and reading the mail she retrieved from the mailbox. His mother loved talking on the phone. When she found her son watching her, she would shoo him away.

Lay would go back into the living room and make sure the front door was locked and turn off the lights in his mother's nursery pretending to be a living room. He would emerge and find his mother with the phone pressed to her ear as she warmed something to eat.

After getting home and feeding Lay his mother might go to her room and plan out what she was going to wear the coming week. She too worked at the same factory his aunt Bree worked at. His mother didn't talk too much about work to Lay, but he figured she did what his aunt did. They worked at the same factory, the eleven year old decided. So, they worked as wire strippers for Johnson Electric Company.

Usually, his mother would get on the phone and call someone and talk until late.

"It's not great work, but it's work and it helps pay the bills," his mother always said about her job.

"Who were you talking to?" Lay asked curious.

His mother just looked at her son steadily.

"How come you don't like your job?"

Lay did not understand why she worked at a job she did not like.

"Some of us don't get that choice, Lay," his mother said with a gentle smile. She stroked her son's cheek. "All the dreams and plans change and there's nothing you can do about it but try and survive."

"But shouldn't you like what you do?" Lay asked, thinking. "You like clothes. Why don't you work with clothes?" He paused and looked at his mother listening but not talking. Her easygoing smile would slowly disappear. "I mean, you could work in a clothing store and get paid to shop or help people buy their clothes."

His mother would get quiet and Lay would stop asking questions.

After eating or shooing Lay out of the kitchen he would head to his small bedroom. Lay's bedroom consisted of a big window that was three feet high and split in two and secured by a hasp. In front of the window was a white curtain. Beneath the window was his bed. To the left of his bed was a dresser and a desk where he piled all of his books and personal stuff. His twin bed was large compared to Lay. On the desk sat his radio. He liked to listen to music from all over the radio dial. Unlike his mother his taste in music was more eclectic.

He would sit in his bedroom and read his comic books with the radio playing just loud enough to hear the drum and bass and humming and singing of soul music. At his age, Lay would have had a hard time naming one artist or song he liked. The music was just background noise for him.

Lay had several drawings of superheroes pinned on his bedroom wall. He collected the entire series of two of the most popular comics and continued to tell his mother his comics would be valuable in the future. His mother never argued, but she did not imagine comics being of any value. His most valuable comic had to be the Batman Damned comic he had bought with his birthday money that became collectible overnight because the artist decided to show Batman's weenie.

On Saturdays, after a night at his cousin's house Lay would wake up and have breakfast with his aunt and usually Hanna or Jordan. Jay would go to work early on Saturdays. He would work until noon. Jay would come home and for an hour or two hang out with Lay.

The two would sit in the backyard and play catch with Jay's football. Lay was horrible at catching and spent most of his time chasing down the football which usually bounced against his hands or chest and away from him.

"Maybe football isn't for you," Jay said with a smile.

"No, I'll get better," Lay said wishing he was better. "I promise."

Saturday afternoons, after leaving his cousin's house, Lay would climb in the car and find bags of groceries in the backseat. His mother always bought groceries before coming to pick up Lay. They would drive down Saint Charles and his mother would try to time the lights and sign along to the music. Lay would sit in the backseat and try and see what his mother bought for the week. It was usually just rice, lettuce, tomatoes, milk and cereal.

His mother would turn right onto Sixth Street and made a hard left into the gravel parking lot and make another hard right into her parking space in front of the window which led to Lay's bedroom. Every time his mother drove him home Lay wanted to ask why he couldn't just climb in through his bedroom window. It would have been so easy, the eleven-year-old thought, but he never mustered the courage to ask.

Instead, he would climb out of the Volkswagen and help his mother with the groceries she bought and carry in anything she needed carrying. Lay loved helping his mother.

A few weeks later his mother might tell Lay something she had been thinking about. He listened as if it was a new idea. "You know I am thinking I should work for the department stores and tell them what to buy," his mother said.

Lay would agree.

"You think they would listen to me? I mean, they probably got all these college educated, rich, white women sitting around talking every day about what is selling and what isn't."

"You should try," Lay said always believing in his mother even when she didn't.

"I mean, they might find that my view of things, though it will be different, might be something that makes sense to black women trying to look good without a lot of money."

"I think that's a good idea," Lay said with a slight grin.

His mother would nod and agree and that would be the end of the conversation and her ideas for the moment.

Lay, when home, would go to his room and draw or listen to the radio or read. When his mother called him, he never thought it was an inconvenience. He loved being around his mother.

"Lay, I was thinking," his mother said in the kitchen with her arms folded in front of her, the phone pressed to her ear.

Lay knew whoever his mother was talking to had greenlighted an idea about how to make the apartment feel more spacious. She would explain the need to rearrange the apartment and ask for Lay's assistance. He would always help his mother. It never seemed a big deal to help her.

She was always smiling and laughing and talking about things with someone on her phone while Lay helped. He just was happy to be near his mother.

After helping his mother Lay would ask to go outside. His mother never wanted Lay to go too far from the apartment. Lay promised.

"Don't throw rocks at the factory," his mother warned.

Once outside, in the sun, Lay usually found himself walking down the walkway away from the street toward the alleyway. As he walked, he would look at the tired chain link fence which separated the apartment complex from the brown wood house of an old white couple.

Lay had seen the man and woman climbing into their old car, but never spoken to them. They did not look friendly to Lay.

Once Lay said, "Hello." But the old man did not even look up.

Maybe, Lay thought, the old man was deaf.

He had learned some people could not hear well in school. Lay had never imagined people could not hear. His teacher had told him and the class every sense could be taken away. That concept was frightening

On Saturday, Lay decided to see if the old man was hard of hearing.

The old man was hunched over by time and old age. The weight of life, Lay always thought, had bent the old man like one of those trees being blown by the wind. He, like the trees, bent instead of breaking after a lifetime of realizing he could not fight the wind or life's struggles.

"Hey," Lay said loudly to the old man. He ran to the end of the apartment complex and the old man looked up, seeing Lay. He smiled and waved.

"Hey," Lay said again, and the old man nodded.

"I'm Lay—Lathan," Lay said. The old man smiled and nodded. That was the extent of Lay's relationship with his next-door neighbor.

When the nameless old man came out of the brown house with a dark wood backdoor and climbed slowly down the back stairs he was always dressed in dark brown pants, a work shirt and heavy shoes. On his head was a brown brimmed hat.

On Saturdays, in the late afternoon, Lay might catch a glimpse of the old man. Rarely did he see the old woman on Saturdays. He imagined she puttered around the house on those days.

If Lay did not see the old man and knowing there were no kids his age in the apartment complex, the soon to be twelve-year-old would just explore.

The eleven-year-old might walk around the apartment complex. There was always something to see near the apartment complex. Behind the apartment sat the great dumpster where all the trash collected until the garbage truck came to empty it.

The dumpster stunk of rotten food, baby diapers, rancid meat, and things Lay did not want to think about. He gave the dumpster a wide berth. Anytime he walked by the big dark blue cannister he imagined something was trapped inside under the hundreds of plastic and paper bags.

Once, feeling brave, Lay had stepped close enough to catch a nose full of the sickening stench and gagged and nearly vomited from the disgusting odors surrounding the dumpster. There was always a brownish liquid dripping from the dumpster when Lay walked past the blue container. He tried not to think what the liquid was draining from the dumpster.

Instead, Lay, once past the dumpster and parallel with the apartment Lay saw the backs of the storefronts which faced Fifth Avenue. There were always half a dozen cars parked in the rear of the storefronts. The store directly across from the apartment house, as best as Lay could calculate, was a currency exchange.

Lay knew the biggest store was on the corner of Fifth Avenue and Saint Charles. The Kentucky Fried Chicken restaurant did a brisk business no matter the day. People parked on Saint Charles to run in and get their chicken. They parked in the rear parking lot and in the alley. Everyone liked KFC. There were always people standing outside of KFC.

Lay did not walk to the chicken corner. There were too many adults on the corner and waiting for wings and drumsticks. Too many adults waiting for anything was a problem to Lay.

So, Lay walked to the end of the apartment complex and turned back toward Sixth Street. As he walked, he took in the factory which sat on the corner of Sixth and produced something Lay knew used plastic and electrical parts. There was a loading dock with a roll down gate. On a workday there were easily fifteen or twenty cars and trucks parked around the factory.

The alleyway which separated the factory from the apartment was wide enough to allow two cars to pass each other easily. Lay would pick up rocks from the gravel drive and pause and recall what his mother told him. He was not to throw rocks at the factory.

He smiled at her words as he threw rocks onto the roof of the factory and not *at* the factory. He might throw three handfuls of rocks onto the roof before getting bored and continuing his apartment explorations. Standing in the gravel alleyway which broke the sidewalk in two for cars and trucks to enter and exit. From Saint Charles all the way past the apartment complex stood the three-story gigantic red brick building which took up a third of the left side of Sixth Street and went all the way to the other side of Seventh Street.

Lay always paused when looking at the three-story building with its faded signage on Sixth Street. Lay could barely make out the name but he knew it said: American Can Company. All the windows had bars on them. Across the street from the alleyway that ran behind the apartment was a rusted rollup door that could allow a semi-truck inside, but in all the time Lay had lived on Sixth Street the rollup had never been raised. The building looked like a prison to Lay, though he had only seen prisons on TV and in movies.

Lay, always curious and inquisitive, never crossed the street and checked the doors or windows of the prison factory. Though curious by nature the eleven-year-old could not explain why he never crossed the street or was not compelled to try to investigate the factory. The factory, unlike the one right behind his apartment, made him uneasy.

He would walk in front of the apartment building and watch the American Can Company factory as if he expected something to happen. He did not know why the quiet building unnerved him, but it did. Lay always felt as if the building was watching him.

Not wanting to stand on Sixth Street under the silent surveillance of the can company Lay never stood on the sidewalk long. Uncomfortable and without any kids his age around Lay would return to his apartment.

His mother would be on the phone talking loudly about everything and anything. Lay would go to his bedroom and turn on the radio, just loud enough to drown out the sound of his mother and read a comic book or three. He might draw or write.

He would have dinner. His mother would eat or not and go into her room on the phone. Lay would watch TV in the kitchen and eat peanuts and drink a soda while he did. When he got tired, he would go to bed. Before going to bed Lay would check on his mother who usually fell asleep in her clothes. Lay would turn off her TV and turn off her lights as he went to his room and to bed.

Sunday mornings, Lay woke earlier than usual. He would slip on a pair of shorts and a T-shirt and take out the garbage. He hated taking out the garbage, but he did it because his mother expected him to pull his weight. Lay would grab the garbage bag in the kitchen and then grab the trash in the bathroom and his mother's room and shove them all in kitchen bag and head to the nasty dumpster. He would hammer toss the trash bag into the open mouth of the dumpster and head back to the apartment.

Lay, back in his apartment, would wash up and dress like he was going to school. He would brush his teeth, use the bathroom, comb his hair and have breakfast, not always in that order. Dressed he would check the clock on the stove and at fifteen minutes until the hour he would go into his mother's bedroom and give her a kiss on the cheek and head for the front door. At the front door Lay make sure he had his house key around his neck, like he did everyday he went to school.

Just three blocks from his house sat Saint Paul Catholic Church and School. On the right side of Sixth Street sat the rectory. It housed a dozen nuns, he was told. On the left-hand side of the street, on the corner, was the pastor's house. It housed Father Pierre and Father Lawrence.

He walked into the school he went to every day and instead of going right and into the school, Lay went left and into the expansive sanctuary. The interior of the church was all stained glass, wood and red carpeting. The pews were wooden and cushioned in red fabric. At the altar was a red-carpet runner which led to the main altar and podium. The podium was wooden and had a crucifix cut into the front of the lectern. Behind the altar was another raised section where the preacher sat in a wooden chair with red cushioned seat and backing. Behind him was a gargantuan wooden cross which had to be thirty feet high and twenty feet across. To the preacher's left was a wooden cabinet with the water and wine sitting on it. A silver cross sat atop a silver container on the cabinet. To the preacher's right was a wooden bench with red padding.

Lay walked down the main aisle of the church and found a seat three rows from the front. He liked sitting there to see and hear all the details and murmurings, respectively.

At the hour, the preacher was led in by two altar boys. One altar boy was carrying a long wooden cross. The other boy was walking and swinging the incense ball and making the sanctuary smell like heaven, Lay decided.

Chapter 3. Jay Beck

Lay loved when Jay would take Lay and Jordan for a walk before dinner. Jay, Jordan and Lay would usually walk to the park and maybe play a pickup basketball game or just watch for a bit. Those moments with Jay were special.

Jay was just so different than everyone else Lay encountered regularly, other than his uncle Joe. Nothing Jay or his uncle Joe said seemed meaningless or thoughtless. Jay and his uncle Joe were aware of the world and Lay knew it. They were his personal oracles and he listened intently to the two elder Beck men whenever they spoke.

"Lay," Jay said one day after coming home from work and going to the backyard to decompress. He sat on the wooden table the family used for backyard cookouts. "You got a girlfriend?"

Lay looked at his cousin amused.

"What you think that's a stupid question?"

"I'm eleven," Lay said looking at Jay confused.

"Yeah, yeah, I know that," Jay said with a small grin. "I sometimes forget." He paused and pulled out a Butterfinger and handed it to Lay. Lay smiled at the candy and began to unwrap it.

"Thanks," Lay said feeling bad he had not said that before unwrapping the candy bar.

"You're welcome," Jay said. "Remember you have to control yourself to control others."

Lay took a bite of the Butterfinger.

"Why did you ask me about having a girlfriend?" Lay asked curious.

"I been thinking that this whole thing is based on trying to impress women," Jay said a little irritated.

Lay did not always speak when Jay finished speaking. He had to piece together what his cousin wasn't saying. He was a high schooler and high school seemed incredibly complicated. Sometimes Jay would say things in the silence. Lay paid more attention to the quiet moments than when he was agreeing or pretending to know what his cousin was talking about.

"Girls are confusing," Jay said annoyed. "They want you to be their protector, but you can't protect them unless they want your protection. It's confusing."

"You have a girlfriend?"

"Jay likes Nonie," Jordan said with a cackle.

Jay looked at his younger brother and did not say anything.

"How did you pick her?"

"I don't know, we just got along," Jay said unsure. He paused and looked at Lay.

"Does she want you to protect her?"

"Sometimes," Jay said bothered. "And sometimes not."

High school seemed difficult. There was always something going on. Jay loved talking about the boys trying to prove they were the baddest at school. He had told Lay about the endless pushing matches which, if someone felt disrespected, resulted in someone fighting. All the pushing and fighting was all over girls. Girls, in high school, according to Jay, were always trying to get boys to fight for them.

"Why?"

"I don't know," Jay said honestly. "I think it is a game to them."

"You ever fight for Nonie?"

Jay laughed in answer. "Fools fights for girls, you ask me. Some girls like the attention. They need the attention. My pops warned me about those types of girls." Jay paused, thinking. "If you are with someone and she's being harassed, that's different, but no. No, I haven't fought for Nonie." He added, "I haven't had a reason to."

Lay listened and filed away what Jay said about fighting for a girl in his memory. He wanted to ask Jay why anyone would fight for a girl. At eleven Lay did not really see any real reason to fight for girls. There were exceptions. He would fight for his mother. He would fight for his aunt. He would... well, he might fight for Hanna. That is where it ended for Lay. His mother, his aunt and Hanna were worth fighting for.

The Fridays and Saturdays on Twentieth were always filled with small moments like Jay walking Jordan and Lay to the park or Jay sitting in the backyard and talking. As school started to come to a close for the summer Lay sat in school and thought of his handful of great moments with Jay.

One day, in the beginning of May, Hanna, Jordan and Lay walked into the house and noticed Jay's things there. Lay looked around the house and not finding him inside went out the backdoor to the backyard and found Jay sitting on the wooden table. He had a liter of Thirst Quencher next to him.

"What you doing here?"

Jay looked at Lay curiously.

"Ain't you supposed to be at the store?"

Jay shook his head. He took a breath and looked at Lay. "I got suspended," Jay said embarrassed.

"Why?"

Jay took a handful of seconds to answer. Lay watched as Jay took another breath.

"One of my friends stole something and I got blamed for it," Jay said annoyed.

Lay didn't say anything. Jay looked at Lay and nodded.

"Yeah, I know," Jay said looking at his shoe tops. "I need new friends."

Jay was holding something in his hand.

"What's that?" Lay said pointing to Jay's hand.

"It's a ring, from...," Jay trailed off. He lowered his head.

"Did you tell your mom?"

Jay snorted.

Lay sat beside his older cousin and appreciated the moment.

Jay slipped the ring into his jeans front pocket. Lay watched out of the corner of his eye. It looked like a silver snake ring, Lay thought.

"So, how long you suspended?"

"Don't know, think it's for two or three days," Jay said reflectively.

Lay nodded.

"Hey, Jay, Hanna says you're in trouble because you keep doing stupid things with your stupid friends," Jordan said from the top of the steps to the back door. The seven-year-old was all smiles.

Jay and Lay looked at Jordan standing in the doorway with his windbreaker tied around his neck like a cape. His big round belly gave him the impression of a baby black Santa Claus instead of a superhero.

Lay smiled at his younger cousin.

Jay turned away from his brother and climbed off the table. He looked around the backyard and shook his head. Lay climbed off the table and stood near Jay.

"You want to take a walk?"

Lay nodded in reply.

The pair headed to the wooden gate that separated the backyard from the hundred-foot strip of grass which ran the length of the property to the sidewalk.

"Jordan, tell Hanna we're going to the park. We'll be back in a while."

"Can I go?"

"No," Jay said needing some space. "You need to do your homework."

With that Jay and Lay walked out of the backyard and down the walkway to the sidewalk. Twentieth at that hour of the day was still pretty quiet. Small knots of kids were visible and walking up and down the streets. The little kids, younger than Lay, were heading toward the park.

"Who's the ring for?"

"Why does it have to be for anyone? Why can't it be for me?"

Lay smiled in response.

"No, I'm kidding. It's for Nonie."

"Why you get her a ring?"

Jay looked at his younger cousin curiously.

"She said that she liked it once, when we were out," Jay said with a smile. "I thought I would get it for her. You know? Show her she's important."

"She doesn't know that already?"

Jay looked at his younger cousin, curiously. He smiled slowly. Jay reached out and playfully pushed Lay away.

"Girls like to feel special," Jay said to Lay.

"Why?" Lay walked beside Jay. "Doesn't she know she's special already?"

Jay was walking at an easy pace and Lay was making two steps for every one step of Jay's when his taller cousin spoke.

"Can we change the subject?"

"Sure," Lay said with an uncertain smile. "Do white people live around here?"

Jay slowed and looked at Lay as if he had just showed Jay he had a sixth finger.

"You ask some weird questions."

"Is that weird?" Lay asked trying to keep up with Jay. "I wanted to ask that a long time ago but never could think of a good time to ask." He paused. "I was thinking about that when you stopped talking about Nonie."

Jay shook his head and sort of chuckled. He looked at Lay and smiled. Lay liked Jay for several reasons but the best reason was he never got angry or frustrated at Lay's questions. Uncle Joe and Jay both had that quality. They never seemed to get annoyed at Lay's curiosity.

"I don't really know where they live now," Jay began. He seemed a little distracted. "I just kind of remember living in the city, but it's really not that clear. There were a lot of white people in the city where we lived. Maybe, that was a dream. I just know that when I first went to Saint Paul's there were a bunch of white people and my mom and dad decided to send me to Saint Matthews so that...," Jay trailed off.

"Yeah, I know, to have a better chance," Lay said with a small smile. He understood the academic theory. College was the way out of Underwood. Public school was overcrowded. Teachers struggled in public schools. In the private schools' classes were smaller and teachers were able to teach. The idea was simple, if you wanted your child to go to college you tried to send them to private or parochial school.

"I was there but it was *too* white," Jay said. "I transferred to Township West." He nodded. "I don't think that happens too often."

The odd pair walked down Oak Street toward the park just on the opposite side of Mannheim Boulevard.

"So, why didn't you work today?"

"The school called and told my boss I was suspended. So, I have two days off work."

"That's cold," Lay said with a twist of his lips.

"It's cool," Jay said with a smirk. "I needed a break."

"Wait, you never answered me about the white people," Lay said realizing he had not got an answer to his question earlier.

"There used to be white people here. I don't know why they left. I just remember when we arrived, they were leaving," Jay said to his cousin.

"Why?"

Jay shook his head.

"Why don't you know?"

"Think that you can walk up and down most of the blocks around here from Mannheim to Nineteenth and there ain't that many white people that live around here."

"Why?"

"Got me," Jay said uncertain. "I think they live in the Gardens and over in Riverside. They have decided to live elsewhere."

Lay paused his questioning.

They arrived at the park and instead of playing basketball, they sat on the climbing structure and watched as a couple of boys in T-shirts and shorts battled on the court like they were trying out for the NBA. The longer boy with the tight fade and "ballislife" T-shirt was good. Yet it was the boy with the diamond earring and the Obey T-shirt who was the real baller. While the two boys were playing three more boys showed up and warmed up. They stripped to their T-shirts and shorts and played aimlessly while the two boys finished their intense game.

"Hey, Jay, you playing?" One of the boys with big ears said, waving to him. "We need one more to run a three on three."

Lay shouldered his cousin to play.

Jay slid down from the climbing structure and made his way to the court. The six boys played three on three. The two boys that had battled were on opposite teams. Obey and Jay were on the same team with the big eared boy who had called Jay over.

The team of Obey, Jay and big ears won the first two games easily and at the end of the third game Jay, sweating like he had just climbed out of the shower, called it quits. He was dripping sweat as Lay, fresh as a daisy, shook his head at his cousin.

"You stink," Lay said making a face.

"Yeah, I was playing basketball," Jay said with a big grin on his face.

"You still stink," Lay said with a grimace.

Jay shook his head and grabbed Lay and wiped his sweat on his younger cousin, against his protests. Jay laughed. Lay pushed away from Jay and when he got free pretended to retch.

"Now, you stink too," Jay laughed.

"I stink of my smarts," Lay said with a laugh.

"What's that mean?"

"What's *what* mean?"

Jay shook his head. "You just say things to say things. Don't you?"

The pair walked back to Twentieth.

"Jay, remember when I was asking about the white people?"

"Yeah," Jay said looking at Lay.

"Why do you think they left?"

"I don't know."

Lay listened. He fell silent.

They were a block from Twentieth when Lay spoke again. "Well, I was trying to think since I been alive if I ever just been around black people," Lay said thoughtfully.

Jay laughed. "That ain't real. We don't get that choice. We got to deal with them all the time. They are everywhere. They our teachers, policemen, firemen, bankers and whatnot," Jay said to his cousin. He paused, thinking. "I think when we first moved here there was three or four white families on the block, up the street, but they moved out a year after we moved in."

Lay listened, thinking. He chewed on the new information. The two walked down the street and passed parked cars.

"Has it always been that way?"

Jay laughed again and turned on Twentieth with Lay by his side. He looked at his cousin curiously. "Seriously? Well, far as I know it's always been that way," Jay said concluded.

Lay nodded, thinking.

"You know there are some whites that never see black people," Jay said with a sly smile.

"Naw, you said that they are everywhere," Lay said looking at Jay evenly.

"Yeah, I did say that, but there are some really rich white people that have so much power they don't even have to see us all their lives."

"Really?"

"I don't know," Jay said with a laugh. "I'm just as black as you and all I know is what I see and read."

Chapter 4. Twentieth on a Friday

As school slowly came to an end Lay did not mind the walk from school with the dozens of other kids who moved up the street. The outsider feeling had disappeared. He did not feel so... out of step.

On Fridays especially there was an added excitement and anticipation as he and the other kids made their way from school and toward home. It was as if, on Fridays, the further away from school the freer the kids felt, and the liberation took hold of Lay as well once he crossed Nineteenth and turned onto Twentieth and spotted Hanna's green and white house in the middle of the block.

Every Friday he spent the night over Hanna and Jay's house. There, in that two-story prairie house, life with his cousins began. Fridays on Twentieth things seemed more colorful, louder and vibrant.

Twentieth was a neighborhood, Lay always thought. Everyone knew each other. There was no tension on Twentieth. At least, there was no tension on Twentieth where Hanna and her family lived.

Fridays on Twentieth with Jay were like no other days in Lay's life. He was this bigger than life character. He never seemed scared or in a hurry. Jay was the first kid Lay knew who had a job. Jay was by definition a young man, and he was Lay's favorite cousin. He liked Jay because unlike Jordan the older Beck boy wasn't moody. He liked Jay because he wasn't Hanna. Hanna was just too bossy.

When the sun finally set Jay, Hanna, Jordan and Lay had dinner with Jay's mother, Lay's aunt, and usually an hour or so after dinner his uncle, Jay's father, walked into the house from work. Jay looked like a younger version of his father; Lay liked to remind his cousin. Hanna looked like a mix of her mother and father. She had her mother's eyes and hips. Jordan looked more like his mother.

Usually, after dinner, Jay called up his friends and went out. He always promised to be home by midnight.

"You know he's getting a car to drive Nonie around?"

"Who's Nonie?" Aunt Bree asked.

"Some girl Jay likes," Jordan said to his mother.

Lay didn't say anything.

Hanna and Jordan were the evening entertainment at the Beck home. Hanna and her mother loved board games and playing cards. So, everyone played board games and cards all night. Occasionally, Hanna coerced her father to play. Those moments, rare indeed, were always so fun. Hanna's favorite board game was Monopoly. She always promised to play Monopoly with Lay and Jordan if her father would play, but that never happened.

Rarely did the family get together to play Hanna's favorite board game, but when they did it was a magical night. In the fifty-three days of summer the Monopoly board came out three times.

The first time everyone played Hanna was the banker and her father oversaw the real estate cards. Lay's aunt did not like to play games, but she did like Monopoly. If she played then her husband, Lay's uncle played. Jay was the crafty one of the family. He was always trying to craft deals between himself and others.

Hanna was the thimble. Lay's aunt was the old shoe. Lay's uncle was the top hat. Jay was always the racecar. Jordan, when he played, always wanted to be the iron or the man on the horse. Lay usually ended up playing with the dog token.

Jordan got his money and immediately wanted to quit. He was so unfocused. He ended up watching TV and falling asleep on the couch while everyone played.

"No one can buy property until they go around the board once," Hanna announced.

"Put five hundred on Free Parking," Hanna's mother said. Hanna, the banker nodded and placed an orange five-hundred-dollar bill in the center of the board.

"Every time we pass Go, we get two hundred dollars," Jay said to Lay.

"Every time we all pass Free Parking, we toss another five hundred in the kitty," Hanna's father said.

"That's it," Hanna said with finality. She quickly added, "If you roll doubles, you roll again. Three times and you go directly to jail."

"One last thing," Hanna's father said, with a smile. "You have to build property equally. You can't have a house on one piece of property and a hotel on the other."

The first Monopoly game began and in six circuits around the board Lay was in trouble. Everyone was giving the youngest player advice. Lay did not know who to believe. They all seemed to want to win.

The money was crazy to Lay. All he had to do was make it around the board and he collected two hundred dollars. Of course, there were all these obstacles getting around the board.

The first time around, after everyone had gone around the board once, Hanna was the first buy property. She bought Vermont Avenue. Her mother bought a Reading Railroad.

Lay bought his first property and thought he was doing something. The first property he owned was Oriental Avenue. He was all smiles, like he had found the keys to a long-lost treasure.

"Don't get excited," Jay said with a chuckle. "It hasn't even got exciting yet." Jay shook his head.

His aunt rolled a five and landed on the Jail. She was just visiting.

Jay rolled seven and landed on Chance. He flipped over the card and found the Get Out of Jail Free card. Jay shrugged and laughed.

"That's good?" Lay said uncertain. Hanna nodded.

Uncle Joe bought Mediterranean and rolled a double. His second roll he landed on Saint Charles Avenue and bought that. Everyone around the board was suddenly excited for some reason.

"If you roll doubles three times you go directly to jail. You have to pay seventy-five dollars to the pot, and you lose a turn," Hanna said to Lay who was still confused when his uncle rolled again and bought Tennessee Avenue. In three rolls Uncle Joe had more property than anyone playing.

Hanna rolled again and bought the Electric Company.

"Hanna, if you want to sell that to me, I'll buy It for what you bought It for," her mother said.

Lay rolled and landed on Pennsylvania Railroad. He bought it.

"Lay, if you want to sell that to me, I'll buy it for what you bought it for," his aunt said.

His aunt rolled an eight and landed on States Avenue and bought it.

Jay landed on Virginia Avenue and bought it. It was his first property of the game.

On her next roll Hanna landed on Kentucky Avenue. She bought the high value property quickly with her five-hundred-dollar bill.

"The game is pretty simple," Jay said to Lay. "All you have to do is pay attention. If you don't pay attention, then you losing money. That's our philosophy. So, make sure if someone lands on your property you call for your cash. Otherwise, if someone rolls you snooze you lose."

Lay rolled and landed on Indiana Avenue. He bought the property to block Hanna's monopoly. Everyone, except Hanna, smiled at Lay's purchase.

"You know you're gonna sell that to me, eventually?" Hanna asked her question really not a question. She smiled evilly with a slight tilt of her head and steady look at her younger cousin.

The next to roll was Lay's aunt and she landed on Saint James Avenue. She immediately bought it and studied the board.

Jay rolled a seven and landed on Kentucky Avenue.

"Pay me," Hanna said like she had been stabbed with a knife.

Jay shook his head and paid Hanna for rent.

Uncle Joe scooped up the dice after Jay paid Hanna and rolled. He rolled an eight and landed on Atlantic Avenue. He bought the property and placed the property card with his other cards.

Hanna rolled a three and landed on Illinois Avenue and everyone, except Lay, shook their heads. Hanna bought the property while Lay's aunt tried to explain what the purchase meant to Lay.

"You have to know that Hanna is going to be on you from now on for Indiana Avenue. She wants the first monopoly. That would make the game tough," his aunt said.

Lay nodded, thinking over the soon to be battle between Hanna and his ownership of Indiana Avenue.

Lay picked up the dice and rolled. He landed on Marvin Gardens. He purchased the pricey piece of property with his orange five-hundred-dollar bill. His Uncle Joe gave him his property card and change.

Jay rolled and landed on Ventnor Avenue. He purchased it and looked from Lay to his father, thinking.

Uncle Joe was the next to roll the dice. He landed on North Carolina Avenue. He purchased the high-priced property.

"That side of the board is for the big power moves," Jay said to Lay.

"Why?"

"Because to own it is one thing to develop it is another," Jay said as an answer.

Lay nodded, not sure he understood. He looked at his dwindling money and hoped he could hold out until he passed Go and collected two hundred dollars.

Hanna picked up the dice and scanned the board, trying to be strategic. She was on Illinois Avenue and suddenly uninterested in any property on the side of the board.

"Come on, Hanna," Jay said impatiently. He looked at Lay for encouragement.

"I want an eight or a ten," Hanna said and rolled.

She rolled a ten and landed on Pennsylvania Avenue. She bought the property.

"Why did she buy it when Uncle Joe owns North Carolina?"

"Well, in this game Monopoly is all about making sure not everyone gets a monopoly," Jay said to Lay. Lay nodded picking up the dice and rolled. He landed on Short Line Railroad. He bought the railroad and suddenly had two railroads.

His aunt rolled doubles and landed on Free Parking. She collected all the money in the pot, nearly six hundred dollars. She rolled again and landed on B&O Railroad. She suddenly held the other two railroads of the game.

Jay rolled and landed on Short Line.

Lay smiled and reminded his cousin he owed him some money.

Jay paid Lay.

Uncle Jo, the leader of the tokens racing around the board, rolled and landed on Park Place. He bought the property with a smile.

Hanna picked up the dice and calculated before tossing the dice on the board. She rolled a five and landed on Boardwalk. Hanna screamed with joy as if she was picked to sing the National Anthem at a ball game.

She bought the most expensive property on the Monopoly board and stared at her father silently.

"You know I am not going to sell you Park Place, sweetie," Uncle Joe said with a smile.

"You think that now," Hanna said with a smile. "But you know you are going to sell it to me. You have to. I'm your Boopie bear."

"Boopie bear or not, I am not going to give up Park Place to anyone," Uncle Joe said.

"Great," said Jay. "Lay it's your turn."

Lay picked up the dice and rolled. He landed on Park Place and understood the value of the two most expensive properties on the board.

Hanna's mother rolled and turned the corner onto the most expensive side of the Monopoly board. She rolled doubles and landed on Pacific Avenue. She bought Pacific Avenue and rolled again. She landed on Chance. The orange card said something about Building and Land Ventures and Collecting $150. Lay shook his head as his aunt put the card face up at the bottom of the deck. She received her money from the bank.

Jay rolled and landed on Mediterranean Avenue. He collected his two hundred dollars and bought the property, suddenly ahead of everyone else.

The game was fast paced. At first, it seemed complicated but Lay seemed to get the gist of it all. Everyone was trying to buy property and stop others from getting monopolies, generally. The game was all about monopolies. The more property you owned the more powerful you were. That made sense to Lay. Of course, it made sense as his money dwindled, and he prepared for the second circuit around the board.

The second spin around the board was filled with obstacles. There were suddenly properties he had to avoid or pay rent. He was on the lookout for properties that were still available as well. For an eleven-year-old the information was not too hard to understand, but it was the pace of the game that took getting used to and understanding. It seemed that everyone playing was moving incredibly fast and predicting each other's moves. So, Lay was often reminded to roll when he was making sure he got paid by anyone landing on his properties.

By the end of the second go round of the board all the properties were gone, and the real Monopoly game began. There were endless negotiations with each dice roll. Hanna wanted Lay's property that would give her a monopoly. At the same time, she was bargaining with her mother for Saint James Place. She offered Jay Water Works for Ventnor Avenue.

In three circuits around the board, he was struggling. His cousins were steadily trying to negotiate for property wherever they landed.

The way Lay saw the game it broke down into two camps. Jay was trying to beat his dad and Hanna and he needed either Indiana Avenue or Marvin Gardens to get a monopoly. Hanna was trying to beat her brother and father.

His aunt was a silent bargaining realtor. She was negotiating properties along the way. Unlike Hanna she tried to work with everyone. On one deal she had bought the Electric Company from Hanna. Hanna did not want it and she got two hundred dollars in the deal. She really wanted to own all four railroads and offered Lay Vermont Avenue and Saint James in exchange for Pennsylvania and B&O Railroads.

The first game Lay's property included Baltic Avenue, Oriental Avenue, two railroads, Pennsylvania and B&O Railroad. He had bought

Indiana Avenue, Marvin Gardens and North Carolina Avenue when things got hectic.

Somehow all the property was bought up while Lay was just trying to pay rent wherever he landed and receive rent when people landed on his properties.

Lay was not a real factor in the game and starting to tire when Jay started bargaining.

"Look, Lay, I'll give you Vermont for Indiana Avenue and three hundred dollars cash," Hanna said with a friendly smile.

"Don't do it Lay," Jay said narrowing his dark eyes and squeezing his lips like he was going to whistle.

"You can't tell him what to do," Hanna said looking to her father and mother. "Tell him he can't try and tell Lay what to do."

Both Hanna's mother and father shrugged their shoulders in response.

"It's not fair," Hanna said pouting. "I just want to break this game apart and Jay knows that if Lay sells me Indiana for a great deal I will win," Hanna said lifting an orange five-hundred-dollar bill to Lay. "You aren't using it. If you sell me Indiana and North Carolina I will give you a thousand dollars." She paused. "That's more than fair."

That first Monopoly game was epic. Lay had sold Hanna Indiana Avenue and Marvin Gardens and two more turns around the board Hanna was a land baron from Saint James all the way to Illinois Avenue. There was no way anyone could bypass Hanna's dominance.

Lay got tired around ten o'clock and before he quit the game, he asked Jay what he should do with his property.

"Okay, the way we play is instead of just giving up your property we have you sell it back to the bank and we have an estate sale and secret bids on each property."

Lay asked for an estate sale. Lay's dog token was placed in Free Parking for the remainder of the game and honored as he left.

"Good game," Jay said with a broad smile.

Chapter 5. Officially Summer

When summer officially began Lay, as usual, met Jordan and Hanna in the rear of the school and walked to their house on Twentieth. That walk, the last day of school, from Saint Paul's was a lot different than all the other walks before. It was a leisurely walk, but a walk full of anticipation for what was ahead. All around Lay were faces he had walked with and initially ignored or who ignored him. In the days and weeks of walking from school to the Beck's he began to recognize faces, if only faces.

Everyone was talking about what they were going to do over the summer. Lay didn't have plans. He walked and listened to the little kids in front of him talking about their plans.

"I think we're going to see my grandparents for a week or two," a little boy not more than nine or ten said. Lay looked at the boy and tried to recall his name. In the two months he had walked from school to Twentieth he hadn't made friends with anyone. There were no boys Lay's age. The older boys walked a different way. The little boys hung out and walked with themselves.

"I have baseball all summer," another little boy, maybe in third grade, said.

"I'm going to an art camp, I think," said another nameless boy.

Lay walked along and tried to imagine what his summer was going to be like. Was he going to go to the Taste? He had always wanted to go to the annual food festival on Navy Pier but for one reason or another never gone. Lay thought as he walked if he could do anything this summer, he wanted to go to the Shedd Aquarium. He had always heard about it but never been. There was supposed to be white whales at the aquarium and if they were Lay wanted to see one. There were also supposed to be penguins at the aquarium.

Of course, going to the Shedd Aquarium meant asking his mom to take him. Lay tried to think of other things he would like to do over the summer that did not interfere with his mother and her busy work schedule.

Instantly, as Lay walked with the dozens of kids following Hanna and her friends, Lay had a list in his head. He wanted to go to the Taste. Every year he wanted to go to the Taste. It was one of the coolest things in the city during the summer. Located in Grant Park it was a foodie's dream. Every food was there. Lay wanted to try a deep-fried hot dog or some of the best deep-dish pizza. Of course, the Taste was in Grant Park and that meant his mother having to take him.

The eleven-year-old thought about his mother, during the summer. She worked during the day and maybe once or twice she might be able to take Lay to the city. He imagined his mother taking the day off and driving them both downtown for the day. That day off would be filled with all the things Lay wanted to do.

As he walked behind the dozens of kids heading toward Ninth Avenue Lay dreamed of going to the Shedd Aquarium. All year, when field trips were offered at Saint Paul's Lay was always disappointed upon seeing that the field trips were never to the glorious Shedd Aquarium. He wanted to go to the Shedd for so many reasons. Lay wanted to see the shark feeding, if he went. There was an exhibit of the Giant Pacific

Octopus Lay had read about while in school that he wanted to visit. He thought about his hopes of going to the Shedd Aquarium, and thought if he went, he heavily emphasized if, he ultimately wanted to go to take a picture with a white whale or a penguin.

Like the other kids around him, Lay marshalled on in his summer thinking. Everyone ahead of him were spinning their hoped-for summer plans. It didn't seem a bad idea to have summer plans.

The rest of Lay's list was all the touristy things he had never done since realizing the city was just a bus or el ride from Underwood. Lay had been born in the city and before he was in school was living in Underwood one of the suburbs west of the city. Just twenty to thirty minutes away the city seemed another world for Lay.

Yet, he imagined if he could do anything that summer, he would like to go to the Water Tower Plaza. He figured if he got to see the Water Tower he and his mom might walk up or down Michigan Avenue. Lay knew his hopes for the summer were small compared to the other kids plans but his plans were hopes, nonetheless.

If the summer was magical and Lay hoped it might be, he dreamed of going to the Lincoln Park zoo. He had been to Brookfield zoo, but Brookfield zoo wasn't Lincoln Park zoo. If he had a choice, he wanted to go to Lincoln Park zoo. Like the Shedd Aquarium, Lay had particular animals and exhibits he wanted to see while at the famous Chicago zoo. If Lay found himself at the Lincoln Park zoo he wanted to see the nearly extinct black rhino. He had learned about endangered species while at Saint Paul's and been fascinated and concerned about the protection of those endangered animals.

If he and his mom went to the city for the day, he would love to go see the Cubs play at Wrigley Field. Lay thought over his list and added two more things he would love to do over the summer. If he could, he wanted to go on a Chicago River Tour in one of those double decker boats that told of all the cool information about the four rivers and how the city reversed the flow of the river and why they did. The final thing Lay wanted to do, to make his summer incredible was go to the John Hancock building. He wanted to go to the observation tower with the see-through floor.

On the other side of Ninth Avenue the biggest group of kids broke off and by the teens there were just about a dozen kids following Hanna and Deanna and Penny. Lay looked around and tried to think what he was going to ask his mother. Three days? Was that a lot of time off? Lay, walked and found Jordan kicking at a tree for some reason.

"Jordan, stop kicking trees," Hanna said looking back and seeing Jordan in mid-kick. The eight-year-old dropped his foot guiltily. He ran ahead and caught up with the ten or so kids still following Hanna.

Three days of going to the city, Lay thought. It wasn't a week with his grandparents or a summer camp. It was just a summer dream list.

Of course, Lay knew asking his mother directly was never a good idea. She had all these ideas already in her head. When he crossed Sixteenth Street, he was still thinking of how he was going to ask his mother about his summer plans.

Hanna and her girlfriends hugged. Jordan shook his head. Lay and Jordan kept walking.

Penny was waiting on Nineteenth for Lay to give him his hand. Lay smiled at the pretty girl with the sprinkle of freckles grabbing his hand and them running across the four-lane avenue.

"Thanks," Lay said with a timid smile.

Penny looked and gave Lay a big smile but did not say anything.

The foursome walked down Twentieth Street and in the middle of the block Penny and Hanna hugged and said goodbye. Jordan was playing with the screen door and waiting for his sister to open the door. Lay sat on the porch and watched as Hanna and Penny separated. Penny walked down the street. Hanna spun on her heels and walked to the porch steps.

"Come on," Hanna said pulling her necklace from beneath her blouse and the front door key dangling there. She walked to the door and unlocked the front door. Jordan pushed in as soon as Hanna pulled the key out of the lock. Lay waited and followed Hanna into the quiet house.

"You're awfully quiet," Hanna said looking at Lay curiously. "You, okay?"

Lay nodded. He took off his backpack and deposited by the couch where he usually slept on Fridays.

Hanna and Jordan were in the kitchen when Lay crossed from the living room to the dining room. Jordan was standing in front of the open refrigerator looking for something to eat. Hanna sat at the kitchen counter and turned on the TV and flipped through the stations trying to find something to watch.

Lay sat in one of the chairs in the dining room and watched as the TV screen blinked from one station to another, thanks to Hanna.

"Jordan, close the refrigerator," Hanna said with a slight annoyance. "You know you aren't supposed to snack before dinner."

The refrigerator door slammed.

"How come?"

"Because you will eat something and that will spoil your dinner," Hanna said adding. "You then will tell Ma that you ain't hungry and late at night you will be complaining about being hungry."

"That's not me," Jordan said, trying to sound innocent.

Hanna didn't say anything else. Jordan stormed from the kitchen and plopped next to Lay.

"What are you watching?"

"Not sure," Hanna said to the back of Lay and Jordan's heads.

"Can we watch Sponge Bob?"

"No," Hanna said with a sour expression.

Lay smiled at Hanna's response.

"Why not?"

"Jordan, school just ended. I am not going to explain how you are not going to sit around and watch Sponge Bob all summer and drive me crazy. You need to read a book or two this summer. You need to do something other than be cooped up inside this house watching TV."

Jordan spun around and glared at his sister, thinking.

"Aren't you in the house right now? Aren't you watching TV? How come you ain't reading a book?"

Lay smiled at Jordan's argument.

Hanna turned off the TV. She climbed off the stool and walked into the hallway where her bedroom was located. She was gone for less than a minute. She returned with a book.

Lay and Jordan looked at the book and back at Hanna as she returned to her seat at the kitchen counter. She slid the TV remote away from her and opened the book defiantly.

Jordan turned around and sat on the loveseat he was sharing with Lay.

"Well, I guess that's that," Jordan said, puckering his lips underneath his broad nose. He looked at Lay and then back at his sister reading her book. "I'm going downstairs to my room to read or play or do something not involving TV," Jordan said climbing to his feet.

Hanna did not look up from her book. Lay watched as Jordan looked at his sister one last time before going to the basement door and heading downstairs. Lay, left with Hanna in the now quiet upstairs tried to think what he could do until his mother came to pick him up.

"Is Jay working today?" Lay asked and got no response from Hanna. Lay sat on the loveseat for a few more uncomfortable moments and then climbed to his feet. He looked at Hanna reading at the kitchen counter. He looked past her to the backdoor and thought absently of going to the backyard. Immediately, he thought better of the idea. He turned on his heels and headed toward the front of the house.

"I'm going to sit on the porch," Lay said grabbing his backpack and going out the front door.

On the porch, Lay opened his backpack and methodically emptied it onto the porch.

Inside of his backpack were eleven ballpoint pens, five broken mechanical pencils, without lead or erasers, just shells really of what they were, seven sharpened pencils, not longer than three inches, three paperclips, twenty-three staples, five notebooks, one three-ring binder and five books he had bought at a book fair and never read. The notebooks were mostly filled with his deliberate and shaky cursive. His math notebook was beat up and curled at the edges. In most of the notebooks were sketches of fantastic birds and fish and every imaginable and unimaginable creature an eleven-year-old mind could create. In the pocket of one of the zippered compartments he found four pink erasers. He tried to recall where and when he had gotten those erasers.

Searching the empty backpack Lay discovered he had several unharmed mechanical pencils. The eleven-year-old smiled at the discovery of the mechanical pencils. For some reason beyond his understanding Lay found himself happy at the sight of those four, no five, mechanical pencils which had survived sixth grade.

He looked at his broken and beaten three-ring binder that looked more like a plastic covered folder than binder at the end of the school year. At some point Lay had broken the three-ring binder and just removed it and used the binder as a sturdy paper holder. Lay thought to throw the binder away but knew better. His mother always liked to go through his backpack at the end of the year and take the papers and work Lay had done and create posters and art from his work. So, though he looked at his work as complete and another step toward seventh grade he did not toss the remnants of the year.

Placing the broken binder on his lap Lay took out a piece of loose-leaf paper and began to write up his summer plans. He did not write in too much detail. He simply wrote the goals he wanted to achieve during the summer. He wrote a list of places he wanted to visit with his mother. Three days he calculated. One day a month Lay imagined. He wrote with the belief that one day a month his mother could take him to Chicago to experience the things he always wanted to experience in the greatest city in the world.

He finished his summer plans and folded it up and wrote on the outside: To Mom. He packed back all his contents of his backpack and once back inside the pack noticed his backpack had two holes in the bottom of it. The binder's edge stuck out of the hole on the left and right. Jamming it into the backpack all year had torn the backpack. Thankfully, the holes were just big enough for the binder and nothing else seemed to have fallen out of his backpack.

When Lay's mother picked him up Lay was hopeful, but not expecting things to change that much over the summer. At least, that was what Lay thought when he climbed into the Volkswagen the night of the last day of school. His mother had already figured out his summer plans.

"Lay, before you get started, listen to me," his mother said as the music played some song about freaks coming out at night. Lay hated that song. It only made him more uneasy at night. The song seemed to suggest to the eleven-year-old that at night anything was possible.

"I am working while you are off. I am not going to let you sit around and get in trouble around the apartment without supervision."

"But I am almost twelve," Lay said to his mother.

"That's true. I want you to see twelve and thirteen and all the years of your life," his mother said. "So, to make sure you do I have arranged to drop you off over Hanna's and you can be there until I get off work. If you want, you can stay overnight not just on Fridays. All you have to do is tell Hanna and she'll call me and let me know."

Lay listened, thinking. "Wait, no, I don't want to stay over there if you are going to be home alone." The boy in the backseat shut his mouth and knew he was a son, but he was also a protector, even if just a little one.

"Okay, so that's settled," his mother said as the Volkswagen raced down Saint Charles. His mother smiled and looked back at Lay. "So, what do you want for dinner?"

"McDonald's," Lay said from the backseat.

His mother laughed at her son's response. Lay loved eating at McDonald's. He loved the endless choices. Yet, the pair rarely drove the four blocks to the nearest McDonald's.

That night Lay and his mother drove to McDonald's and sat in the drive-thru lane and ordered. Lay ordered two cheeseburgers, fries and a chocolate milkshake. His mother ordered a hamburger, fries and a Coke.

Lay and his mother ate their fries as they drove back to the apartment. Once inside the pair sat in the kitchen, at the small kitchen table, and ate and laughed and talked about Lay's summer on Twentieth. Lay was ever excited about the possibilities of being on Twentieth with his cousins. He would laugh all summer at the antics of Jordan. He would learn to get along with Hanna. The bonus of being on Twentieth was the endless chances to talk to and hang out with Jay.

He had some friends on Twentieth as well. Unlike Sixth Street there were kids his age on Twentieth as well. On Sixth Street there were kids he did not know and did not seem to want to know him.

Chapter 6. Soul Review

Lay recalled in the middle of the summer going to see his uncle and his band perform at a hall on Fifth Avenue near Greenwood.

It was a little past noon when Fred Clark showed up in his van. He was dressed like he always was anytime Lay saw him, boots, jeans, T-shirt, work shirt. Lay loved how tall Clark kept his Afro. Around his neck was a gold chain and a gold ring. On his finger was a thin gold band.

"What up little man?" Clark asked with a toothy grin. He called everyone "little man." He was easily the biggest person Lay had ever met. His hands were enormous. He had huge arms and a thick chest, like he was a weightlifter.

Behind Clark, appeared the whip thin Perry. He was a mustached man who always seemed brooding and or sad about something. He had said three words to Lay in the dozen times they bumped into each other. So, that Saturday, Lay did not expect Perry to say anything, and he was not disappointed when the man dressed in sneakers, jeans and a T-shirt did not recognize or say a word when Lay watched them enter the house.

A few minutes later Donald Baker rang the front doorbell, and his uncle opened the door to see his friend. He was a friendly man with a mustache and beard and dressed in casual shoes, khakis and a short-sleeved shirt. Baker and Uncle Joe hugged and headed basement door. When Baker saw Jordan and Lay, he paused just long enough to say, "Hey" before following Uncle Joe downstairs.

After the band had arrived, they were packing their instruments and equipment up the stairs and to Clark's van parked in the alleyway. Jordan and Lay watched as they carried the heavy speakers to the van. In an hour the band was driving away.

The Becks and Lay piled in the car and Aunt Bree drove. Hanna sat next to her mom. Jay and Jordan sat on either side of Lay. Lay sat in the middle of the Pontiac Vibe as Aunt Bree drove through the streets of Underwood listening to everyone talking about the upcoming show.

"I hope that Larry and Aidan are there," Jay said to the window.

"Who are Larry and Aidan?"

"Two losers that Jay hangs out with," Hanna said from the front seat.

"They're not losers," Jay said annoyed.

"Think they'll have cotton candy there?"

"Jordan, you need to be good tonight. Everyone needs to be good tonight. Your daddy's trying to make his dream come true. We're going to support him," Aunt Bree said as she drove down Madison Street toward the eastside of Underwood. Lay looked from the center of the car out of the window as the neighborhood became more familiar to him. He noted the street numbers decreasing and was almost ready to scream when he saw Sixth Street. They passed Sixth Street and turned right on Fifth Avenue and drove a few blocks to a yellowish square building with a flagpole in front of it.

Aunt Bree parked the Pontiac Vibe in the still relatively empty parking lot, and everyone climbed out. Lay dressed in a T-shirt and jeans dug his hands in his pockets as Jay and Hanna walked toward the front of the building with their mother and Jordan trailing behind.

"You any closer to buying your car, Jameis Oscar?" Hanna said with a smirk, from the front seat to Jay.

Jay looked to the front of the car and at Lay. He looked up and in the rearview mirror was Aunt Bree's eyes.

"I'm really close," Jay said reluctantly to Hanna. "I only need about another hundred before I buy my car and stop hitching with the family Partridge."

Lay listened but did not say anything. He just tried to keep up with the battling Becks.

The hall was just a few blocks from Greenwood and Lay lingered on the street looking at the distant township. It looked like Oz to him. The streets looked wider. The houses seemed bigger. The cars seemed cleaner. Just two blocks away.

The pair turned the corner of the building and found there were about twenty or thirty people standing outside talking and laughing and eating. Hanna, leading the charge, walked up to the table where a plump woman the color of molasses with short curly hair and dressed in a bright blue T-shirt that said: Staff over her heart was sitting beside a woman the color of a dark pecan, with gold half-moon earrings dangling from her ears.

"Hi, I'm Hanna Beck, I'm on the guest list," Hanna said confidently.

The woman had long eyelashes blinked her big eyes and studied Hanna and Jay and Lay, as Aunt Bree and Jordan walked up. The woman tilted her head to the right seeing Jordan and Bree.

"Breonna Herbert, is that you?"

Aunt Bree looked up and there was an immediate recognition. The two women laughed and smiled and hugged.

"Girl, I am just back from Atlanta and doing my cousin a solid, manning the door," the nameless woman said louder than necessary. "I haven't seen you in some years."

"We need to catch up," Aunt Bree said. She and the woman exchanged phone numbers and suddenly all the Becks were in the VFW hall.

"How you know her?" Jordan asked, curious.

"We went to high school together a long time ago," Aunt Bree said.

The hall was three stories, including the basement. The main floor was where the stage was set up and there were about twenty round tables set up on the floor with a twenty-foot square area marked off with stanchions for dancing when the live performances began.

There was food in the rear of the building. All the Becks headed to the food to eat. Lay followed. They had spaghetti, hotdogs, hamburgers, cheeseburgers, salad, chips and ice cream. Everyone ordered what they wanted and because they hadn't opened the doors to the general public as of yet their food came almost instantly.

"You stay here," Aunt Bree said to Hanna and Lay, and she and Jordan walked backstage. Jordan, who had a hotdog in one hand and a canned soda in the other smiled as the pair disappeared backstage.

"What's back there?"

Hanna was eating some chips and did not answer. She was looking around the big space for anyone to talk to other than Lay when she saw someone she knew. She waved. The other girl waved back. With that Hanna wandered off with some friends of hers.

"Don't trip, Lay," Jay said with a silly grin on his face. "Just sit here and enjoy the food, the people and the show."

Jay and Lay ate at the same table but Jay vacuumed up his food and was gone before Lay had time to finish his spaghetti. Jay was drinking his soda and scanning the crowd when he stopped and Lay looked in the direction his cousin was but could not see anything unusual.

Jay climbed to his feet. "I'll be back," he said and with that Jay disappeared into the small crowd.

Lay sat and ate spaghetti and then he ate his hotdog while people streamed into the hall. There were tables all around Lay and people sat and talked and ate. As tables filled up Lay finally finished his hotdog and thought about going to find Jay. Instead, he sat and opened his bag of corn chips. While he was eating other kids sat at the round table with him, but none spoke.

Having just had a handful of chips Lay climbed up from the table and decided to eat outside. He carried his can of soda and opened bag of chips through the building crowd of people and paused at the exit. Lay looked back at the stage which seemed to be now so far away between him and the crowd of people standing, talking and the three rows of tables on either side of the hall. People pushed into the hall as Lay stood near the doors.

People were laughing and talking as Lay slipped out the door. In the cool of the late afternoon which was quickly becoming night Lay watched as cars moved up and down Fifth Avenue. A group of girls dressed in fluffy dresses and shiny shoes were near the door when Lay stepped outside. Two boys dressed in collared shirts and dress pants were smoking near the corner. They looked at him and did not smile as they studied Lay. Lay, standing on the sidewalk, moved in the opposite direction of the two boys on the corner.

The two boys, Lay turned back to look, had not moved from the corner. He was relieved of that. He just wanted to walk and breath in the slightly cooler air outside of the hall.

Lay was walking to the end of the block when Jay came around the corner with two of his high school friends. They were dressed in jeans, T-shirts and sneakers.

Seeing Jay instantly made Lay exhale the uneasiness. Jay seeing Lay smiled and nodded.

"What are you doing out here?"

Lay did not speak. Jay was not listening. He reached down and cuffed Lay by the back of the neck and turned him around and walked him back into the hall. Lay reached out and put a hand on Jay's hand and the older boy released him with a smile.

"You know you shouldn't leave the hall?" Jay asked, but it wasn't a question. He looked at Lay with a smile.

Lay looked up and noticed in the lights of the street and cars Jay's eyes were a little red for some reason. Instantly, Lay wondered had Jay been crying? Was he sick?

"You, okay?"

"Yeah," Jay said with a crooked smile.

Lay looked back at the two boys following. They too had goofy smiles on their faces and their eyes looked bloodshot. Lay knew he should know what was going on with all three boys, but the answer eluded the eleven-year-old. That bothered Lay.

He wrestled with the problem. Jay and his two friends are acting goofy. Jay isn't always goofy. Jay is usually serious. Maybe it is being around his friends that makes Jay goofy. But what makes them so goofy?

Lay was trying to figure out the goofiness problem when he started hearing the sound of music and singing. Once inside the hall Lay could see onstage a group of people playing instruments and a kid wearing tight pants and no shirt singing into the microphone.

People, in the auditorium, were standing watching and eating and listening as the band ended and the shirtless boy walked off stage.

Jay walked Lay through the crowd and through the round tables where they had eaten earlier and near the stage stood Hanna and some other girls. Lay walked toward Hanna and the girls. He looked back for Jay and found he had once again disappeared. Lay considered fighting his way back through the crowd. He simply stood near Hanna and on the outside of the circle of girls.

Onstage the emcee, a fat black man with a short Afro Lay had seen before at other city events, was on the microphone. He was a round faced man with no visible neck dressed in a paisley-colored shirt, black slacks and boots.

"Give it up for Baby Boy and Shockadelica. I cannot believe he is only sixteen," the emcee said showing off a gap-toothed smile. "He was something else, trying to do his own version of Prince and Michael Jackson all in one." The emcee danced around on stage robotically and licked at his hands and fingers as he did a little pantomime. The crowd laughed at the emcee.

"All right, I know none of you came to see my chocolate loveliness," the emcee said with a toothy smile.

"That's right," someone said from the crowd. The crowd laughed at the heckler.

"Tommy? Is that you? Boy stop playing." The emcee looked into the crowd of faces like he knew who had spoken. He smiled and turned his attention back to the crowd gathered. "We are so proud to introduce this next musical group. They are some of the hardest working musicians you have ever seen and are about to hear. They got together to remind everyone of the smooth sounds of bygone years. Give it up for the sounds of Soul Review."

Lay stood near the side of the hall. The curtain parted. Hanna and her friends clapped and screamed as the stage lights shone on the Soul Review. Lay clapped too. Many in the crowd clapped while some talked and some ate.

Lay's uncle, dressed in a suede coat with fringes on the arms, had his back to the audience when the curtain opened, and he spun around. He was wearing boots, tight black leather pants, a leather belt with a gigantic belt buckle and a colorful silk shirt unbuttoned almost all the way to his belly button. Lay smiled at the sight of his uncle. He was always dressed in work clothes when Lay saw him after work. This look was a little shocking.

The Soul Review were the guys, the old friends of his uncle who came by and every once in a while, Lay got to hear play. Most of them worked with his uncle, but that night they seemed so different onstage.

There was gigantic Afro of Clark three times bigger than he usually wore it. The Afro was swaying back and forth to the beat of the drums as the drummer began alone. He was transformed into a thick necked dark brown man wearing sunglasses and a pirate hoop earring in his earlobe. He was wearing a silk colorful collared shirt opened to show off his muscles. Clark made the drum kit sound like a slow-moving engine of a train.

On either side of Lay's uncle were two dark men with guitars, wearing colorful silk shirts, dark jeans and boots. The one with the six-string guitar had a headband, sunglasses and moved back and forth on the stage nervously. Lay recognized the nervous guitar player as the wannabe Rockstar Perry with a dozen gold chains around his neck.

Perry ever quiet, as if on signal, played his guitar and accompanied the drums. He played along and led the drum sound down the tracks.

The other guitar player, younger and with a mustache and beard seemed more confident. He spun around to the crowd and flashed a Chesire Cat smile as he played the four-string guitar with mostly his fingers and thumb. Lay recognized the younger guitar player as Baker. The showman played to the crowd.

In the rear of the stage was a thick woman who reminded Lay of one of the women on TV, but he could not recall the woman he thought she looked like for the life of him. She was wearing sunglasses and bobbing her head to the music. She was standing behind the synthesizer with two Afro puffs, wearing a silk blouse. Lay figured the silk shirts connected them. Lay knew the woman. She was Delilah Raymond and was a piano teacher when not onstage.

They began with a crowd favorite song about sitting on the dock of the bay somewhere. The tune was catchy. As Lay's uncle sang people around the hall sang the catchy hook with him. By the end of the song the crowd was singing and dancing along.

Soul Review's second song, led by Lay's uncle, moved into a cover of a familiar song by a singer who had hundreds of hits according to his mother. In seconds after the song began everyone around Lay was singing.

He looked around and saw people standing and singing and smiling. He was smiling and singing as well.

"We're having and party, dancing to the music," Lay sang and was surprised to hear his voice lost in the sound of others.

"If you take requests, I have a few for you," his Uncle Joe sang, and the crowd just seemed hypnotized by the song and music behind it.

"Having a Party" was one of his mom's favorite songs. She played it anytime she could. Lay knew all the words. It seemed so did most people in the hall. They sang along to the song as his uncle held the microphone and crooned.

His Uncle Joe sang the crowd favorite by Sam Cooke. As Lay sang and listened to his uncle he heard the similarities in his uncle's voice to the legendary singer. The eleven-year-old could only shake his head at the realization. His uncle had a good singing voice. He pumped the microphone in front of him like it was a water handle, Lay recalled.

His mother showed up by Lay's side for the end of the second song and the beginning of the last song.

"We want to thank you all for all your love and attention. This is our last song," Uncle Joe said into the microphone.

There were boos and cries against it.

"We love you for that. But this last song is for a very special person who has stuck with me through thick and thin. My rock. My love. My wife."

The Soul Review began their last song with a more soulful song than the first two, Lay decided. It was a song he had heard before and took him a few minutes to recall. His mother, standing by Lay, just rocked back and forth like she was being moved by an invisible hand one way and then the other.

"Oh she may be weary, Them young girls they do get wearied, Wearing them same old shaggy dress, yeah, yeah," Uncle Joe sang. His voice was deeper, raspier and full of pain and hurt.

Everyone was swaying back and forth like they were on a boat and Lay thought it was a strange song to end with but when the song was over everyone clapped and whistled and clapped some more.

"My baby brother is pretty good," Lay's mother said to everyone around her. Lay smiled at his mother clapping and laughing and pointing to the stage.

Lay smiled and blushed at his mother's antics. He didn't know why he was suddenly flush and hot, but he was. He smiled and tried to listen to the song and the music.

"That's my baby brother," his mother said, her voice almost a scream.

At the end of the Soul Review's show Hanna and Jordan ran onstage and hugged their dad, while everyone clapped.

The VFW had more acts and Uncle Joe and Soul Review stayed around and signed autographs and soaked up the adoration. Lay's mother pushed through the fans and stood in front of her younger brother with her hands on her hips. Uncle Joe climbed to his feet.

The two siblings hugged.

"You did it," Lay's mother said to her brother. "You really did it." She shook her head. "You are making your dreams come true." She was suddenly crying for some reason. "I'm so proud of you JoJo."

The two hugged again and Lay's mother kissed her baby brother on the cheek and wiped it away before turning and walking away with Lay trailing behind her.

His mother and Lay drove from the hall home and his mother was all smiles that night.

"Why were you crying?"

"I'm proud of my baby brother," his mother said as she weaved in and out of traffic along Fifth Avenue.

"Tears of joy?"

"Yeah," his mother said.

They drove back toward Sixth Street.

"Mom, you ever play Monopoly?"

"No," his mother said. "Well, I played it when I was a kid, but that was a long time ago."

"What was your piece you played with?"

"I liked the top hat or the racecar," his mother said.

"You ever play as the little dog?"

"I liked the little dog," his mother said with a smile.

Chapter 7.Satchel Paige

As the summer stretched out and Lay got used to his new routine. He spent most days at his cousin's house. He would be dropped off after breakfast and by lunch eat a peanut butter and jelly sandwich or a hotdog or whatever Hanna decided the three of them would eat for lunch. Sometimes, on rare occasions they got Fritos. They always had Kool-Aid or a soda. When the ice cream truck came by Jordan would beg for money and Hanna never gave in. Jay would come home after two, usually, and a few hours later his mother would show up. Hanna would disappear, usually to her bedroom or down the street to Deanna's or over to Penny's.

Dinner at the Beck's was always an event. Occasionally, Jay would have to go and get Hanna from Deanna's or Penny's and Jordan and Lay always tagged along.

Deanna lived on Seventeenth. Seventeenth Street was only a few blocks from Twentieth but In Underwood it was like arriving on the other side of the world. People looked at Jay, Jordan and Lay like they were barbecue chicken or something and wanted to eat them.

"Why are they looking at us like that," Jordan asked.

"I don't know," Jay said. "Maybe they're hungry."

Deanna's house was one of those three story houses with a wraparound porch that looked like it should have been on the East Coast rather than in Underwood township. Jay would walk up to Deanna's front door and ring the bell.

Deanna or her little sister would answer the door and Jordan and Lay would just wait on the walk for Hanna to come out of her best friend's house. If Hanna wasn't over Deanna's, she was usually over Penny's.

The best part about Hanna being over Penny's was the fact that Hanna was only three blocks away from Jay's house. Unlike Seventeenth, Jay knew mostly everyone on Twentieth. He waved to people and said hello to boys and girls Lay had never seen before.

Walking to Penny's house Jay always laughed and smiled.

"How you know Penny's family?" Lay asked as he tried to keep up with Jay. Jordan was skipping along and close.

"Everyone knows the Thompson family," Jay said as he walked. "They are local legends. Two of Penny's brothers broke football records in high school. They went to college only to crap out because of one thing or other. Key, the youngest brother, plays basketball at my high school and if he doesn't screw up could go to college and maybe the pros. He's incredible. Really talented."

Jay looked at Lay and then to Jordan.

"Jordan, don't try and be cute and repeat what I said."

Jordan stopped and looked confused.

"Promise."

"I promise," Jordan said.

"So, we've sort of grown up with the Thompson family," Jay said to Lay. He added, "The boys in the family are trying to keep Key focused and concentrating on being a student athlete. He's got potential."

A block later Jay, Jordan and Lay were standing in front of the red brick house with white trim. In the driveway was a Dodge Charger with its hood up. Two big muscular men wearing T-shirts and jeans were sitting on the stone steps to their front door. One looked like he might be the size of two humans.

"What's up Jay?" The smaller giant closest to the street climbed to his feet and walked toward Jay. He was the color of sand with dark brown French braids in his hair. He had brown eyes beneath thick eyebrows and a slightly bent, broad nose above his wide mouth.

"What's up Mall?"

"Jay," said the bigger giant from the steps to the porch as Jay walked up.

"Everything good?"

Mall closed the distance, meeting Jay in the middle of the walkway. He and Jay hugged and stepped back, and the pair were gripping each other's hand. Mall opened his hand and Jay did too. They slapped hands and nodded. They both smiled.

"You here for Hanna?"

Jay nodded. Jordan and Lay walked up to the giant standing on the walk.

"Is that Jordan?"

Jordan looked at the giant curiously.

"How you know my name?"

"I was around when you was born," Mall said with a smile.

Jordan shook his head.

"Naw," Jordan said with a shake of his head.

"Seriously," Mall said. "Tell your mom hello from Jamal."

Lay tried to walk past Jordan and the giant. The giant extended his thick arm and stopped Lay's progress. He stepped to the side and Jordan walked down the walkway behind his brother.

"Who are you, youngblood?"

"Me," Lay said swallowing when the man spoke to him. "I'm Lay." Lay looked at Jay talking to the bigger giant on the steps of the red brick house. "I'm their cousin."

"Lay," the giant said. "That's a funny name."

"It's short for Lathan," Lay said with a little grin.

"Welcome Lay," the giant said.

"Penny, tell Hanna her brothers are out here," the great giant on upper steps to the porch said. Jay leaned against the steps of the porch and waited.

"Clee, how have you been?"

"Surviving, baby boy," the great giant said, sounding like thunder.

"Heard you working at UPS," Jay said with an approving smile.

The great giant nodded from the porch.

Lay sat on the steps and found the two biggest humans he had ever seen impossible to look away from. They had hands, arms and shoulders like Lay, but nothing like Lay. He imagined they could pull trees up by the root without much trouble. Lay was trying to screw up the courage to ask the giants something when Hanna appeared.

Behind Hanna was Penny, dressed in blue jeans, a baseball T-shirt that read: "Baby" and sneakers. Her hair, during the summer was a red and brown mushroom of curls piled atop her heart-shaped face.

Seeing Hanna, Jay pushed off the porch and gave a wave as Mall and Clee, the biggest giant. The two giants smiled. Penny waved as Lay and Jordan fell in step behind Hanna.

"Why didn't mom call?"

"She didn't need to, I suppose," Jay said as he and Hanna walked back down Twentieth Street and to their home. "Sometimes, she just needs a break, you know?"

Hanna and Jay stopped talking.

Jordan and Lay followed silently.

For most of the summer Lay found himself in the Beck bubble. Everything he did was with one or more of the Beck's. His favorite memories were with Jay. He never had as much fun with anyone in the family as he did with Jay.

Jay was just fun to be around. He was older, but not as old as Uncle Joe. He always said things to Lay that made him think It was... refreshing.

One day, with Jay packing up and getting ready to go to work Lay saw where the board games were located. He walked Lay to the front door and then to the porch.

"Hey, Lay, be good and when I come back, I'll hook you up with a Butterfinger," Jay said walking down the porch steps and to the sidewalk. He walked up the street toward Oak.

Lay liked Jay trying to give him advice, like a big brother. Jay was his cousin, Lay knew, but it felt good to get advice from the high schooler.

He walked back into the house and sat down at the kitchen counter. Hanna had left and Jordan was downstairs doing God knows what. His aunt was in the kitchen preparing dinner even though it wasn't even noon.

"Lay, what you doing today?"

"I don't know," Lay said unsure. "Maybe, I'll sit around and read a book or look at TV," Lay said uncertain.

His aunt busied herself preparing a meatloaf in the kitchen. While she was busy, he decided to pull out the Monopoly game. Lay did not feel like being outside and looked over the Monopoly board. He found the rulebook and read it. He was bored and was surprised at the information.

A few days after reading about Monopoly Lay met Cass.

Cass was this red brown boy with black wavy hair, big ears, big eyes and a thin gold chain around his neck. He was just a year older than Lay, who seemed ten years older behind his dark eyes. Cass lived near the end of the block closest to Oak Street.

The first time Lay met Cass he had a baseball and glove and no one to play with.

"You want to play catch?"

"I don't have a glove," Lay said omitting the fact that he couldn't catch anything but a cold.

"You can borrow mine," Cass said.

They played catch on the sidewalk in front of his cousin's house. Lay borrowed Cass's glove and was horrible catching. He could sort of throw better than catch. The two boys laughed and threw the ball and Cass chased down the errant throws until someone called Cass home.

"Thanks," Lay said giving the kid named Cass back his baseball glove.

"Yeah," Cass said, and he ran off, back up the block toward his house.

From that impromptu catch game, the two boys became fast friends. Whenever Lay arrived at his cousin's house and Jay was not around Lay would go outside and look for Cass.

Sometimes he was on the block.

Usually, the two boys would sit on Jay's porch or Cass's porch and go through the baseball cards Cass had traded for the week before.

"Okay, the way it works is that you get a baseball card right and it is meaningless. Who is this guy, you think?" Cass said, explaining about trading baseball cards. "But then you notice that you got this nobody's Rookie card. Is he valuable? Nobody knows. It's a crap shoot." Cass smiled. "The thing is there are some really valuable Rookie cards."

"How do you know?"

"No one knows. It's a guessing game."

Lay let the conversation drag.

"So, right now I'm trying to get all the Rookie cards for the Cubs from 2016, the year they won the World Series," Cass said with a nod.

"Why?"

"I think it will be a cool collection and maybe valuable. I mean, imagine if I had all the Rookie cards from the 2016 World Series it has to be valuable. I mean, think about it."

Lay listened and thought about what Cass was saying. It didn't make that much sense to Lay.

Cass switched to his favorite topic and favorite baseball player, Satchel Paige.

"You know Satchel Paige would probably destroy most batters today. He was a beast," Cass said.

"Why you like him so much?"

"Well, I guess because my brother told me how Satchel Paige sort of appeared and took the Negro League by storm. He was this incredible player who could pitch, field and hit. He was the first Negro League player considered for the major league, but they selected Jackie Robinson because of... he was hot tempered. Satchel Paige was the oldest player ever to play in the major league. He was the first black player to pitch in a World Series. I think he won two World Series and was selected to three or four All Star games." Cass paused, thinking. "He was amazing."

"He died?"

"Yeah, in 1982," Cass said.

Lay listened. He smiled at the box and then at Cass. Cass got quiet.

"How'd you get into baseball cards?"

"My brother took me to a game," Cass said with a smile. "We went and while I was there, I saw these box sets," Cass said. "I couldn't afford the boxes, but I could get a couple of cards from it." He paused. "That's how my collection started."

That conversation ended with Cass being called home. Lay got picked up by his mother. He returned to Sixth Street.

The weekends had changed thanks to Cass. Friday was still fun with his cousins and uncle and aunt, but Saturday was special after Jay went to work. Lay would go outside and look forward to seeing and talking with Cass.

The two boy's friendship grew and over the summer it morphed into a friendly competition. When he wasn't in Jay's house he was on the sidewalk or in front of Cass's house waiting. They were close friends. They were fast friends.

When he was on the block, they played catch. When they didn't play catch Lay learned about baseball cards. Cass loved baseball and baseball cards.

One day Cass showed up with a big smile on his face and wearing a backpack. Lay knew Cass never wore a backpack. No one wore backpacks during the summer.

"Why you wearing that?"

Cass just smiled and shucked off the backpack and sat on the Beck's porch in the shade and smiled even more.

"I got something and wanted to show you," Cass said finally as he unzipped the backpack and gingerly removed a package in bubble wrap. The package was, as best as Lay could tell the size of shoe box, if it was cut in half and a little bit more. Lay looked as Cass unwrapped the package and revealed a green and brown box that had a brown faced baseball player on the side wearing a white and red baseball uniform and matching baseball cap.

"What is that?"

"It's my Negro League collection," Cass said with pride. He turned and presented the thick box of one hundred and ninety cards in their collectible box.

Lay did not dare to touch the box. Instead, he simply looked as Cass lifted it and allowed Lay to see all the sides of the six-sided box.

"Is that Satchel Paige?"

"Yep," Cass said with a broad smile. "He's my favorite."

Chapter 8. Cass Garrett

One Saturday Lay walked out onto the porch and there was Cass with a basketball in his hand.

"You want to go shoot some hoops?"

The pair walked to the park.

Cass was a really good basketball player compared to Lay. He was a year older and nearly a foot taller than Lay. He could dribble behind his back and Lay was reduced to just watching as Cass tried to score.

"Okay, let's play to five," Cass said and for the first time, since they had left Twentieth Cass seemed to loosen up. "You can take it out first."

Lay knew how to play basketball but was not very good. He dribbled with both hands every so often. He sometimes ran with the ball.

"You trying to hustle me?"

"Hustle you? What's that mean?"

"You know pretend like you ain't something you really are," Cass said.

"Who does that?"

"All sorts of people," Cass said.

Lay laughed. "No, I ain't trying to hustle you."

Cass laughed at Lay.

When Lay shot the ball, it rarely hit the rim or backboard.

Cass would get the rebound and dribble to the rim and Lay was helpless to stop him. He stuck his hands out but Cass just went the other way and scored.

They played for nearly an hour trying to score five baskets.

It was just fun. Lay did not take the game too seriously. Cass seemed focused on scoring five baskets before Lay. Near the end of the game Lay scored his first basket to Cass's three.

"Dammit," Cass said.

"What's wrong," Lay asked, concerned.

"Nothing," Cass said, taking the ball and concentrating to sink his fourth basket.

The game ended with Lay losing by three points.

"You like basketball?"

"Yeah," Cass said. "Why?"

"You just seem mad," Lay said concerned.

"I just thought I would beat you five to nothing."

Lay laughed. "Five nothing? I ain't that bad, am I?"

"You ain't that good," Cass laughed.

The two boys laughed and once they returned to Twentieth Lay said goodbye seeing his mother's Volkswagen parked at the curb. He ran to his cousin's house and found his mother sitting in the kitchen drinking coffee and talking with his aunt.

"Here he is," his aunt said with a smile on her face.

His mother turned and climbed to her feet seeing Lay. She grabbed him and hugged him like she hadn't seen him in years. Lay hugged her back.

"You, okay?"

"Yeah, Ma," Lay said. "Why?"

"I just thought you might be," his mother trailed off. "I am glad you are fine."

"I just was shooting baskets at the park," Lay said.

One Friday night in the middle of the summer Jay came home from being with his friends and found Lay watching TV in the dining room. The house was quiet. Everyone had gone to sleep. Lay was sitting quietly watching the TV when Jay entered.

"How are you still up?"

"I don't know," Lay said with a shrug of his shoulders. "I couldn't sleep and found this weird TV show on and there was a lot of kicking and fighting."

Jay sat down beside his cousin after grabbing something to eat and watched the end of the Kung Fu film with Lay. At the ending Jay could not help but smile.

"When you start knowing about Bruce Lee?"

"Bruce Lee?"

"Yeah, the hero of Chinese Connection," Jay said to his little cousin.

Lay shrugged his shoulders.

"You telling me you didn't know you were watching Bruce Lee in Chinese Connection?"

"I just was flipping through the stations and came upon it," Lay said with a thin and awkward smile.

"What did you think?"

"I don't know," Lay said unimpressed. "I mean, it started out one way and it was all about this gang trying to take over the school. I didn't understand why anyone would want to take over a school."

"Focus," Jay said to Lay.

"The fights were crazy," Lay said with a grin.

"What did you think of Bruce Lee?"

"Who? Oh, the main guy who was fighting," Lay said pausing. "I guess he was okay."

"Bruce Lee is a master, a real master," Jay said his enthusiasm bubbling to the surface. Lay looked at Jay a little curiously.

"He do his own stunts?"

"Yes," Jay said shaking his head.

"Like Jackie Chan?"

"No, not like Jackie Chan," Jay said instantly frustrated. He balled his right hand to stop himself from cursing at Lay. His cousin was only eleven. He didn't know he was slandering the greatest martial artist ever to grace the silver screen. Jay took a deep breath and tried a different tact. "Bruce Lee was before Jackie Chan. If anyone was trying to be anyone it would Jackie Chan trying to be like Bruce Lee."

"Okay, if Jackie Chan and Bruce Lee fought who would win?"

Jay closed his eyes to his cousin's question.

"Bruce Lee did things no one else had seen before. He sort of made Kung Fu a big deal."

"Ain't Kung Fu always been a big deal?"

"No," Jay said frustrated. "Bruce Lee brought all the martial arts out. I guess before Bruce Lee there was Karate and Ju-Jitsu and some other stuff but Bruce Lee combined street fighting and martial arts." Jay paused. "Bruce Lee perfected the one-inch punch. He was a Kung Fu master. There are just so many things that Bruce Lee did, while he was alive, that others were not able to do."

"Like what?"

"He combined Western fighting styles with Kung Fu and created a hybrid of the fighting style no one had seen before." Jay paused, thinking.

"You said that," Lay said impatiently.

Jay climbed off the couch and grabbed Lay by the shoulder. "Come on."

The pair walked downstairs to the basement of the Beck's home. The basement seemed half done. There were pipes and cables dangling overhead. There was a beam that Jay had to duck under as he walked to his bedroom. Lay looked down and noticed the floor of the basement was unevenly poured cement. In front of Jay's bedroom door was a drain that led to the center of the earth as far as Lay was concerned.

Jay pushed open his bedroom door and snapped on the light and the small rectangular bedroom came to life. The room was maybe eight feet high. Jay didn't seem to notice. Lay looked around the room he had never been invited into before.

There was a walk-in closet right next to the door. A lamp was sitting on a small table near the doorway. Overhead were two hanging lamps. There was a bar on the left side of the room. There was one small window in the far end of the bedroom maybe six feet off the ground. The small twin bed was against the wall. Against the wall, just underneath the small window, at the foot of Jay's bed was Jay's desk where a big screen monitor sat. Jay walked to the monitor and turned it on. Lay followed. He looked and cataloged the dozen posters on the wall.

There were three basketball posters of Michael Jordan doing what Michael Jordan could only do. There was Jordan jumping from the free-throw line. There was another picture of him shooting the game winner. There was the iconic shoe poster.

There were four football posters of Walter "Sweetness" Payton. Lay smiled seeing those posters. Sweetness, like Jordan, was a Chicago sports legend. He was the reason the Chicago Bears had won a Superbowl. Every poster Lay had ever seen Sweetness was always caught juking someone out of their socks. Lay admired the classic poster of Sweetness holding the ball like a loaf of bread. There was a poster of him hurdling over some tackler on the other team. Jay had a Sports Illustrated poster of Sweetness in the middle of the air. The fourth poster was entitled Sweetness.

There were three movie posters. One poster was of the film Blues Brothers. One poster was of the film Risky Business. The last poster was of the film Ferris Bueller's Day Off.

Lay smiled at Jay's love of all things Chicago. Jay had told Lay that all three movies had been filmed in Chicago.

The only posters not tied to Chicago sat near the small window of Jay's bedroom. Those two posters were of Bruce Lee. One of the two posters was of the film Enter the Dragon. The second poster was a picture of Bruce Lee punching out, but unlike all the others this poster had words on it. "Do not pray for an easy life, pray for the strength to endure a difficult one."

"Sit down," Jay said sliding out the chair and sitting down. He fiddled with his computer and the monitor blinked on. Lay looked around Jay's bedroom and sat on Jay's bed.

While Jay fiddled with his computer and monitor Lay just looked around his cousin's bedroom. He had about twenty books stacked on the bar. Lay tried to read the titles, but he couldn't.

"You like football?"

"I don't dislike it," Jay said to Lay.

"You play in high school," Lay said looking around the room.

"Naw, I tried out, but I didn't make the team."

"What position did you want to play?"

"I thought about wide receiver or tight end, but there are some really good kids at our high school." He paused. "I should have tried out for defense. No one wants to play defense."

"Is high school hard?"

"Why you asking?"

"I'm just curious," Lay said honestly. "It seems like everyone wants to hurry up and get there, but at the same time they don't want to go."

Jay nodded. Jay's computer blinked on and he was scrolling through page after page of cars and car accessories.

"Is that the car you want to buy?"

"Yeah," Jay said with a smile inching across this face.

"What is it? I mean, what kind of car is it?"

"It's a Pontiac Solstice," Jay said stopping his scrolling. "I am trying to get a oh eight, nine or ten."

"Why do you have so many different cars?"

"I am looking for the best price and trying to get a Targa top, but they only made Targa tops in the last two years of the production," Jay said admiring the car.

Lay did not say anything. He tried to decipher what Jay had just said. He had no idea of what his cousin was talking about.

"My mom has a Volkswagen," Lay said in answer.

"Yeah, I know," Jay said with a smile. "I looked at Volkswagens, but I want to make people look at me like I'm something when I pull up."

Lay opened and closed his mouth silently.

"You know I got two more years in high school and want to go out with a flourish."

Lay listened and did not respond. He was curious but unsure what to say to Jay. He took a deep breath and looked at Jay a little confused.

"Is high school scary?"

"It can be, but it can be sort of cool at the same time," Jay said to his cousin.

Lay noticed Jay had a baseball bat in the corner of his bedroom and was about to ask him a question when his cousin spoke.

"Look, this is Bruce Lee. He is the master. If you know anyone that can do half the things he did, when he was alive, I don't know nothing about them," Jay said and pressed play.

Lay pressed pause. He turned and looked at Lay.

"You try out for the baseball team?"

"I did my Freshmen year," Jay said looking toward the bat in the corner of the room.

"What else did you try out for?"

"Well, my dad boxed a little and I tried out for boxing since he trained me, but I wasn't really that into it." Jay paused. "Hey, I brought you down here to educate you about Bruce Lee, not talk about my failed sports career." Jay forced a smile.

Lay looked at Jay for an instant and turned back to the computer monitor. He pressed play.

For about ten minutes Jay and Lay sat in silence as the video highlighted an incredible fighter who could do two-finger push-ups. He could kick above his head. He moved so fast that several times the video showed his actions in slow motion to capture his devastating power. Lay watched and was amazed by the skill, power and speed of Bruce Lee.

When the video ended Lay turned and looked at Jay who was smiling like he had won a race.

"I think he could beat Jackie Chan," Lay said curious.

Jay shook his head.

"Who knows about this guy?"

"Everybody," Jay said with a smile pointing to the computer and the website where the video was found.

Lay smiled and nodded.

"It's kind of crazy to think that everybody talks about Mike Tyson like he was the baddest man ever," Lay said thoughtfully. He paused. "You think Bruce Lee could beat Tyson?"

Jay smiled but did not answer the question.

"What about Jet Li?"

Jay did not answer.

"What about that guy in Blood Sport?"

"You watched Blood Sport?"

"Yeah, I watched it," Lay said silently proud. "That guy was amazing."

"Jean Claude Van Damme?"

"That was his name," Lay said with a smile. "You think Bruce Lee could have beat that Jean Claude Van dude?"

"Lay, you asking me things that no one knows. I showed you the best of Bruce Lee. He is the best of the best. Everyone was trying to be him. There was no one better at the time. Now, there are all these people who have heard about him and want to be better than him." He paused. "It's kind of hard to compare someone who had no one to compare himself to at the time. I mean, look at Michael Jordan. When he came into the league there was Magic and Bird. They were good. He eclipsed them. At the time no one was close to him. Same with Sweetness. Well, there was Gale Sayers. He was probably the best running back the Bears ever had before Sweetness. But before Sweetness showed up every running back was compared to Gale Sayers."

Lay nodded. Lay rubbed at his eyes, tired.

Jay smiled seeing Lay trying to muffle his yawn.

"Go to bed. You know you ain't a night owl," Jay said shooing Lay from his room and into the half-done basement. Lay walked and noticed that Jay's bedroom outside had the same wood panel that was inside. He wondered if his Uncle Joe had made Jay's bedroom himself.

He walked to the stairs and climbed up the two steps that put him on the landing to the practice room on the other side of the basement and to his left the twenty-four stairs to the main floor of the house.

Lay climbed up the stairs and opened the basement door to the silence of the Beck home at nearly midnight. The house was eerily quiet. Lay blinked and knew as soon as he put his head on his pillow, he would be fast asleep.

He slipped on his pajamas and laid down on the couch and tried not to think too much about Bruce Lee, high school and Jay's search for a car. Lay wondered before he fell asleep if Jay would give him a ride in his new car when he got it?

Chapter 9. Hanna in charge

A few weeks later, that summer, Underwood was stuck in a sticky heatwave. It was late July, and the heat was bearing down on any and everyone foolish enough to be out in the peak hours and when the sun finally set the heat did not break. If people moved, they moved in the cool of the day but by ten o'clock few people were on the streets. For five to six hours a day in late July the streets were deserted, and the sun and heat forced people to find air conditioning. Most chose to stay indoors or in the cool of shade rather than face the unrelenting heat.

Under the same roof, Hanna and Jordan smiled and seemed on the verge of beating each other up at any moment. Lay never knew the cause of the friction. It just bubbled up from nowhere and suddenly Jordan was angry and pouting and Hanna was looking like she wanted to throttle her baby brother. Even in the heat of the day, sometimes Jordan refused to go to his room.

"Hanna, me and Lay are going outside," Jordan said beckoning to his older cousin, showing him, he had two cans of soda.

Lay did not want to go outside but he didn't want to be up under Hanna either. So, he followed his cousin into the heat of the backyard. Stepping out of the backdoor Lay was hit with the wave of heat.

"Jordan, it's too hot to be out here," Lay said with a frown.

"I know," Jordan said simply. "Come on, we can hide out in the garage. There's a radio in there and it's cool in there too."

Jordan crossed the backyard and walked to the small garage door and opened it. Lay descended the back steps and crossed the backyard to the garage door. Lay walked into the darkened garage reluctantly.

Jordan tapped the electric garage door opener by the door and opened the garage door only to stop it halfway up, so that there was a little light flashing in from outside but not all the heat. In the two-car garage sat Aunt Bree's silver Pontiac Vibe. Next to it was an empty spot for Uncle Joe's SUV Lay had ridden maybe three times?

Jordan looked around the interior of the garage and walked to the wall where two folding chairs were hanging. Lay followed. He grabbed a folding chair and opened it and placed it next to Jordan's chair.

Handing Lay one of the soda cans Jordan stepped to the wall and turned on a small radio plugged into a wall outlet.

"You got a station you like?"

Lay shook his head, no.

"Okay, let's listen to WGCI," Jordan said and turned up the radio and sat down in his folding chair.

The music was staticky but audible.

"You know Hanna can be too much, sometimes," Jordan said sitting comfortably in his chair and looking at the half-opened garage door. There was a three-foot opening that afforded a twelve-foot-wide view of the white stones and gravel that composed the alleyway outside of the garage. Lay knew that to the left of him, if he was outside the garage, he would see the wooden fence that butted against the edge of the garage and went another thirty feet to the edge of the property and to the garage of the neighbors. On the Victorian apartment side of the garage was a ten-foot bit of wooden fencing that meet with the chain-link fencing that separated the Beck's property from the gigantic footprint of land where the apartment sat.

"Sometimes she acts like she's my mother. Sometimes. So, sometimes I got to get out from under her," Jordan said, surprising Lay.

"Wait," Lay said confused. "What?"

"Jay tells me that all the time," Jordan said with a laugh. "I just like coming out here and listening to music and dancing and not having to listen to people tell me what to do," the eight-year-old said.

Lay blinked and studied Jordan, confused.

Jordan danced and shimmied and laughed as the music played and the DJ talked about how hot it was and how hot it was going to be that day.

"If you got air conditioning then get up under it," the DJ said. "If you ain't got air conditioning you might want to make some friends with someone that does."

"It's early," Jordan said looking around. "We can hide out here until it gets too hot," he continued. "By lunch we go back in get something to eat watch a movie and when Hanna starts being Hanna bossy boss then we come back outside."

"That's a good plan," Lay said impressed with Jordan.

So, the pair sat in the cool of the garage until Hanna called them in for lunch. Aunt Bree was in the kitchen when the two boys entered the house.

"Wash your hands and come and get something to eat," Jordan's mother said.

Jordan and Lay went to the bathroom and washed their hands. Jordan ran into the kitchen and sat beside his mother. Hanna sat at the kitchen counter with Lay. They had turkey sandwiches, chips, a pickle and apple juice. Jordan got a chocolate chip cookie. Lay got an oatmeal raisin cookie.

After lunch, Jordan asked his mother if he and Lay could watch TV.

"That's fine," she said, looking to Hanna. "I have to go and see Rose, she asked me to pick something up for her from the store." Aunt Bree looked at the three in the kitchen. "Hanna, need you to hold down the fort for a couple of hours. I should be back by four, no later."

"I got this Ma," Hanna said with a smile.

Jordan and Lay were watching some silliness on TV when Aunt Bree came from her bedroom and reminded everyone she was leaving.

"All right Ma, I got this, you go check on Rose," Hanna said with certainty.

With that Aunt Bree left.

"What is wrong with Miss Rose," Jordan said, curious.

"Think she is not feeling well," Hanna said to her brother.

"Is she going to be okay?"

"I think so," Hanna said with a nod. Hanna looked at Jordan curiously. She smiled at his stalling tactic.

"So, what are you two going to do the rest of the day?"

"You're looking at it," said Jordan with a smile. He paused and added, "I might get another bag of chips or a cookie, but this is it."

"Nope and nope," said Hanna. "This is the summer. You are either playing or studying. Playing helps strengthen your muscles. Studying helps strengthen your... mind."

"It's too hot outside," Jordan said with a slight whine in his voice.

"Okay, the choices are simple. You can watch TV for another hour. Then you can either go outside and be a kid or grab a book to read," Hanna said with authority.

Jordan did not respond.

Lay thought over the choices. He liked the idea of sitting in an air-conditioned house and reading a book. Maybe, he could read a couple of the books he had found in the bottom of his backpack from the bookfair that year.

Jordan sulked in front of the TV. The pair sat in front of the TV for an hour. After an hour Hanna grabbed the remote from Jordan and clicked off the TV.

Jordan spun around and stared daggers at Hanna.

"What are you going to do?"

"I'm reading and getting ready for high school," Hanna said with a smirk.

Lay climbed to his feet and walked toward the front room. He made a quick detour and went to the bathroom. He washed his hands and went to the front room and looked at the five books he still had in the bottom of his backpack. There was a book about a boy in love with a girl, but all these obstacles thrown in their way. Lay did not want to read that. There was a book about a man with a brain disease trying to do something good before he died. Lay put that one to the side. It seemed action packed. There was a book about the future where there was a yearly battle to prove who was the toughest. Lay looked at that book and liked the creepy cover. The last book was about high school and some kid trying to prove himself. Lay grabbed the last two of the books and walked back toward the kitchen.

Jordan elbowed Lay. Lay looked at Jordan annoyed. Jordan gestured for them to leave.

Jordan climbed to his feet and waved at Lay. Lay reluctantly followed his younger cousin, pausing only long enough to drop the book about high school in front of Hanna.

"You might like it," Lay said with a smile. "I picked it up at the bookfair," Lay said as an explanation. He shook his head. "But you are going to high school. I'm just going to seventh grade."

Hanna looked at the book.

Jordan stormed out of the backdoor and Lay followed.

In the cool of the garage Jordan turned up the radio and danced and laughed and sang along with the radio as Lay tried to read his book from the bookfair.

The pair were in the garage until Hanna called them inside. It was nearly four o'clock when they re-entered the house.

"Is Jay home yet?"

"No," Hanna said looking at Lay.

"Where's Ma?"

"I was about to tell you that mom called and said that she was going to meet dad at a restaurant in Woodlawn," Hanna said with a slight smile. "They went out on a date," Hanna said her smile broadening. "They do that every once in a while."

Jordan pushed past Hanna and turned on the TV.

Lay stood in the kitchen with Hanna.

"Don't you think that is... romantic?"

Jordan twisted his lips under his round nose trying to think of a good answer.

"So, what are we going to eat?"

Lay smiled at Jordan's question. Hanna turned and dismissed Lay without an answer to her question.

"Well, Ma left me money for dinner, just in case, when she went to see Rose," Hanna said with a grin. "So, what do you guys want for dinner?"

"Pizza," said Jordan from the couch. He was watching Black Panther for the hundredth time.

Hanna looked at Lay. Lay shrugged his shoulders.

"Pizza it is," Hanna said to the boys. "Lay, go to the coupon drawer and find all the pizza coupons. Ma left me a twenty and we have to have enough to feed you, me, Jordan and Jay."

Lay walked to the kitchen drawers and searched for the coupons. He found a drawer with a bunch of coupons inside and pulled out a handful and looked for pizza coupons. He found six pizza coupons. He handed the coupons to Hanna and replaced the other scraps of paper back in the drawer.

Jay arrived a few minutes after Hanna called for pizza. He went immediately to his room to change out of his work clothes. He dressed up in a clean collared shirt, clean jeans and his nice sneakers.

"You ain't eating with us?" Jordan said, seeing Jay all dressed up.

"Got a date with Nonie?"

"Going out with friends," Jay said sheepishly. "Think we're going to see a movie." He looked at Hanna. "Tell mom and dad that I should be home by midnight."

Jay turned and rubbed Jordan's head for luck. Lay walked his cousin to the front door and watched him as he stepped out. Jay looked back and seemed a little surprised to see Lay there.

"Be good," Jay smiled. He walked off the porch and to a waiting car.

Lay closed the door when Jay climbed into the car and the car drove away.

With the absence of Jay, Lay and Jordan suddenly seemed deflated.

"Who wants to play Connect Four?"

Jordan and Hanna played Connect Four. After Hanna beat Jordan two out of three games, she took on Lay.

Lay was no expert at Connect Four but he sort of knew the broad strokes of the game. Jordan was watching and giving advice. Lay listened and ignored everything his eight-year-old cousin suggested. The first game ended in a tie.

During the second game of Connect Four and while they waited for the pizza there was a sound of loud pounding like someone was banging on the front door with a tree and then screaming and laughing and all sorts of random noise outside.

"What's that?"

Hanna, curious, ran to the front and opened the front door and looked out. Jordan and Lay followed.

Hanna stepped onto the porch and Jordan turned on the porch light and pushed past his sister on the front porch. Lay was close behind.

There was a fury of activity in front of the Beck house. There were two boys on bikes on the sidewalk watching Hanna, Jordan and Lay. Lay was sure it was Ricky and Rayshon. Behind them, on the street, on his bike was Cass looking up and down the street for something.

Without notice the three saw Reg go running past the front door and jump over the far porch rail toward the Victorian apartment in the darkness. Behind Reg came Eli and Darryl. Hanna stepped into the path of the two boys who stopped halfway up the steps of the porch.

"Where do you think you're going?"

"Hanna," Darryl said, running into Eli who stopped halfway up the porch steps.

"Hanna," Eli said, bumping into Darryl.

"We're playing Chase," Eli said, attempting to avoid Hanna's searing stare.

"I said, where do you think you're going?"

Eli looked passed Hanna in the direction Reg had gone before he vaulted the porch railing and disappeared into the dark.

Jordan ran to the rail of the porch to watch Darryl. Lay stepped onto the porch and looked at Hanna blocking Eli's progress and Jordan. He stepped to the railing and watched as Darryl ran into the darkness, cutting across the grass in the front yard and through the eight-foot-high hedges used as a fence and border of the property.

"Darryl, just ran through the hedge," Jordan said alarmed.

Lay, Jordan and Hanna focused on Eli. He smiled and backed down the steps from the porch. Once on the walkway he ran down the walkway and then cut across the front lawn following Darryl.

Jordan and Lay watched all the activity from the porch as a group of boys ran around in the dark and through the streetlights avoiding one another. Some of the boys were on BMX bikes. It was chaotic.

"What are they doing?"

Hanna looked at Jordan and then Lay suddenly annoyed.

"They playing Chase."

"What's Chase?" Asked Jordan.

"Two groups. One on bikes or not chasing the other group not on bikes until a certain time. It's fun. Well, it used to be fun."

"You played?"

"Yes," Hanna said with a smirk. She waited until the boys moved down the street a bit and then tried to usher Jordan and Lay back inside.

The two did not seem ready to go back inside.

"They let girls play?" Lay said with a look of disbelief.

"Anyone can play that can hide and make it to the steps of one of the houses on the block picked for safety," Hanna said recalling the game.

"You played?" Jordan said, unbelieving.

"When I played, I was never caught."

"You don't play no more?" Jordan said confused.

"I am too old for that now," Hanna said with maturity. "Chase is for kids. After a while we grow out of that kind of stuff."

At that moment the pizza delivery man arrived. He was driving a stylish four door with a lighted sign on top. He jumped out of the car and ran around to the passenger side and pulled out the pizza container. He walked up to the porch under the three kid's eyes.

"Pizza delivery," the young man said.

Chapter 10. Ice cream truck

A few days later, in the backyard, Lay finally asked Jay if what Cass said was true.

"Well, I don't know if there are hustlers around here," Jay said amused at the idea. "Think mostly everyone is just black and trying to survive." Jay paused. "Who told you that?"

"Cass," Lay said embarrassed.

Jay did not say anything for a minute.

"What are you thinking about?"

"Well, you know I know pretty much everyone on the block," Jay said to his cousin.

Lay nodded.

"Well, be careful with Cass and his family," Jay said thoughtfully.

"Why?"

"They... can be... difficult." Jay took a breath and said in a low voice, "They like to steal."

"What?"

"Just be careful," Jay said to Lay.

"Why?"

"I don't know, really," Jay said to his cousin. They were sitting on the table in the backyard. Jordan was running around with a bubble gun and squeezing out small and large soap bubbles.

Lay listened, thinking.

"Ain't nothing to think about, Lay," Jay said firmly. "People steal every day."

"It's wrong."

"Nobody said it was right," Jay said to the eleven-year-old. "But sometimes the rules are wrong. The laws are wrong. The whole thing is wrong and...," Jay trailed off. He looked at Lay seriously. "It's just how some get by."

"It don't seem right," Lay said confused.

"Right? Right?" Jay shook his head. "The whole right versus wrong thing is where they get us."

"Who?"

"The white people," Jay said, annoyed. He was suddenly very serious. "I know you know about all the black men and women killed by police," Jay said looking at Lay with his big brown eyes. "Is that right?"

"Yeah, no," Lay said, hesitantly. "But I thought they were killed because they had done something bad," Lay said innocently.

"Maybe, some did, but some didn't do nothing but be black and in front of a white or black cop." Jay looked at his younger cousin evenly. "Is that right?"

Lay didn't answer.

"It's like we're playing checkers and they are playing chess," Jay said.

"What?"

"It doesn't matter. All you need to know, right now, is this," Jay said, seeming to hold back all his anger. He pointed to the back of his hand. "That's all you have to be to get got nowadays," Jay said with a nod of his head. He paused. "Just be walking, talking, playing, or driving while black."

"No, you're wrong. The cops ain't like that," Lay said defensively.

Jay laughed. "They like to pretend like they ain't like that, but they like that. They can't be trusted."

Lay fell silent.

"Don't fall for the Okie doke," Jay said to Lay. "They try to blame us for getting killed. The cops will lie in your face and kill you and everyone you love without thinking about it."

Lay opened and closed his mouth without words.

Jay paused. He looked like he was wrestling with a big idea.

"Okay, listen, you need to understand things. The real truth is that just because you and me are black we are seen by everyone as criminals first. In school they try to blame us and punish us because we remind them every day of their evil. Don't let them make you grow up too fast. They try to make us boys' adults quicker than anyone else so they can kill us and say we are armed and dangerous."

Lay swallowed and listened.

"But," Lay began only to trail off.

"It's a cold game we in. We been put in this unfair situation and not given the rules. We are the underdogs and the whole game seems rigged to destroy us."

Lay listened.

"You ever watch TV? Well, if you watch TV then you will see how the white world sees us. We are criminals, pimps, drug dealers."

"And athletes or entertainers."

Jay smiled at Lay.

"No, black athletes are criminals and wife beaters and all the things they can throw at them to make them unlovable when they mess up. The same goes for the entertainers. They use them and throw them away penniless and broke."

Lay winced.

"We ain't doctors, lawyers, plumbers or anything whites are on TV," Jay said pointing to the monitor.

"Why?"

"You asking me? Well, I figure they don't want us to see ourselves the way they see us. I mean, they in charge of all the TV shows and theaters. So, they good with us singing and dancing and being athletes, but once we open our mouths about anything that ain't sports or entertainment that's it." Jay paused.

Lay shook his head.

"You know they love to march out Martin when things go bad. They don't want us angry and tearing up their stuff." He paused and looked at Jordan shooting soap bubbles with his soap gun on the limbs of one of the three trees in the backyard. "I think that's their plan. My dad said that when they want something they the first to tear something up. We the only ones they tell to calm down. They give us a little and then take what they gave us away." Jay paused and rubbed his chin. "We still ain't a part of the we in the We the people."

Lay shook his head, confused. "Jay, all I asked you was if Cass was right about blacks pretending, they poor just to make fun of us behind our backs. I just want to know that."

"I answered that. I'm not sure. All I can say is that there are a lot of pretenders everywhere. You have to pick your friends correctly. Just because they look like you don't mean that they out for you. All you have to do is look at a black and a white cop the wrong way and you might not make it home."

"What's the wrong way?"

"Hell, if I know," Jay said with a shrug of his shoulders.

"I'm telling ma you are cussing," Jordan said with a smile. He was near the back porch steps and shooting soap bubbles toward the sky.

"Hell, ain't cussing. It's in the Bible."

Jordan pouted in response.

"You," Jay said tilting his head at Lay. "I'm surprised no one had this talk with you before," Jay said with a smile. "You ain't a threat yet. You still don't look like a killer."

"What about me?" Jordan said, suddenly behind Jay with his soap bubble gun.

"Well, Jordan, if you go out of the yard and you see a policeman drop that bubble gun," Jay said to his younger brother. "I don't want to hear them say they thought you were carrying an Uzi or something."

Lay did not want to believe his older cousin, but Jay had never steered him wrong. He was always honest. He was always willing to answer any questions. Yet, Lay did not want to believe what his cousin said. It seemed so unbelievable.

A few weeks later Lay was sitting on the porch watching Jay trim the tall bush on the side of their house. He was wearing a pair of shorts, a T-shirt and some beat up sneakers. He was on an A-frame ladder that was only five or six feet tall. Jordan was supposed to be holding the ladder for Jay, but he was suddenly all jumpy hearing the ice cream man coming down the street.

"Jordan, you don't just run away from the ladder," Jay said annoyed at his younger brother who was on the sidewalk and then running into the house to get some money for ice cream.

Lay climbed off the porch and walked to the ladder where Jay was trying to not have to jump off with the electric trimmer.

Jay looked down and smiled at Lay.

"Thanks," Jay said with a smile.

Lay nodded.

"I'm going to get a rocket pop," Jordan said as he blasted out of the front door with money in his hand. Hanna was close behind. She did not look happy.

Lay turned and waited for Jay to finish trimming the hedges.

"Jay, you want anything? Mom told me to ask," Hanna said walking down the porch and to the walkway.

"Maybe a soda," Jay said with a tilt of his head.

Lay smiled and laughed.

"It's an ice cream truck, stupid," Hanna said with spite. "They got ice cream."

"Well, maybe get me a push pop," Jay said with a crooked smile on his face.

Hanna stood in the middle of the walkway and looked at Jay and Lay.

"What? You asked," Jay said with a smile. "I figured you were treating."

"I'm not treating," Hanna said correcting Jay. "Mom's treating." She looked at Lay and smirked. "And what about you?"

"What about me?"

"What do you want?"

Lay was slightly shocked to be included.

"Don't look all surprised," Hanna said to Lay.

Lay looked from Hanna and back to Jay.

"Tell her what you want," Jay said climbing off the ladder with the hedge trimmer.

"Something strawberry," Lay said quickly adding, "Please. Thank you."

Hanna shook her head and walked to the curb in front of their house where kids were already gathering. She looked down the street. Lay looked at Jay.

"What? You didn't think we would leave you out? Did you?"

Lay didn't answer. Jay handed Lay the hedge trimmer so he could fold the ladder up. Jay hefted the ladder over his shoulder and began to walk to the rear of the house. Lay awkwardly followed trying to hold onto the hedge trimmer which was still plugged in. The pair walked toward the backyard fence and the trimmer's cord stopped just a few feet from the stairs of the porch.

"Hey," Lay said in protest, looking back and realizing the trimmer was still connected to the power cord.

Jay looked back amused as he paused just long enough to smile and open the backyard fence.

"Stay right there. I'll be right back," Jay said and Lay watched as his cousin walked to the garage and entered it with the ladder on his shoulder and in a minute, he came out unencumbered and with a silly grin on his face.

"How did you not notice that the trimmer was still plugged in?"

Lay did not respond. Jay just pushed past his younger cousin and quickly unplugged the trimmer from the power cord. Lay was suddenly able to move. His first move was to lift the unwieldy trimmer for Jay.

Jay grabbed the trimmer and walked down the side walkway with Lay in tow to the garage. Jay entered the cool and dark garage. Lay stopped at the doorway to watch his cousin put the trimmer on a hook on the wall of the garage.

That afternoon after the ice cream truck rode away everyone sat and got quiet and enjoyed their ice cream. Jay had a red, white and blue rocket ice cream pop. Hanna had a chopped nut chocolate dipped ice cream cone. Jordan had a Sponge Bob ice cream that was dripping all over him. Lay had his strawberry push pop.

The four ate their ice cream on the porch and watched as Jordan made a mess.

"Can you at least pretend to be interested in eating your ice cream and not making a mess?" Hanna said exasperated at Jordan completely covered in SpongeBob ice cream.

Hanna climbed to her feet and went into the house. She returned with half a roll of paper towels to clean up Jordan. She looked at Jay and Lay and gave them each one square of paper towel and took the dripping mess of SpongeBob from Jordan.

"Want to go to the park?" Jay said climbing to his feet.

Lay climbed to his feet.

Jordan looked at Jay and Lay and Hanna grabbed an armful of Jordan and walked him into the house.

"We'll be back in a bit," Jay said as he walked off the porch with Lay in tow.

Jay and Lay walked to Oak Street and turned left toward Mannheim. It was still hot and there were few people out as Jay and Lay made their way to the park.

"Think we should get something to drink?" Jay said as they walked down the street. Lay did not have money. He never had money. So, he just followed.

Instead of going to the park Jay turned right and walked to the corner store at Mannheim and Saint Charles. For some reason there was a gigantic mural on the wall of the corner store by a local graffiti artist. Lay could not help but smile at the cartoon sprayed there in such rich colors.

The two walked inside the dark store and Jay looked around and found the refrigerator where there were cold drinks. He grabbed two cans of soda.

The man behind the register looked at Jay and then Lay and said, "That's two dollars."

Jay slid two dollars to the man and grabbed the drinks and handed one to Lay as he exited.

Back in the sun and heat Jay walked back to the park. The basketball court sat empty and without an ounce of shade. Jay looked around the small park and walked to the corner of the park where there was shade. A tree cast shade across the foot of the park where there was a sand box and four horses bolted into the ground. Jay sat on one of the horses and the horse rocked forward with his weight. Jay had to reach out and steady himself as the horse threatened to buck him off.

Lay smiled. Lay's smile broadened and made him rewind the image of his cousin almost get flipped off a kiddy horse ride. Lay giggled. The giggled quickly turned into a chuckle and then he was laughing at Jay.

"That wasn't funny," Jay said recovering from his near tumble.

"That was funny. You didn't see it," Lay said with a broad smile. He imitated the clumsy actions of Jay on the horse.

Jay smiled.

"All right, it was sort of funny," Jay said with a laugh. "I almost got tossed off a kiddy ride."

A few days later when Jay came home from work Lay was waiting with a question.

"Jay, you remember when you got suspended?"

"Yeah," Jay said with a nod of his head.

"Remember you said you would help me get better at dribbling," Lay said reminding Jay.

Jay smiled.

"What do you want Lay?"

Before Lay asked he replayed that whole day over in his head.

Jay, Jordan and Lay went to the park to play basketball. Jordan never played basketball. He just loved walking around with his brother. Lay couldn't blame him. He too enjoyed being around Jay.

That day Jordan got the chance to dribble the basketball to the park and he was having a great time.

"You know if there was a sport where all you had to do was dribble," Jay said with a laugh. "Jordan might be king."

When they arrived at the park though Jordan did not want to play basketball. He climbed on the climbing structure. He played on the swings.

Jay and Lay played and Lay knew he was no competition for his cousin. Like Jordan he liked dribbling, but he also liked shooting the ball even if he rarely sunk any shots against his towering cousin. Jay was okay as a basketball player but no superstar. He just happened to be nearly six foot tall and seventeen.

Lay enjoyed not being on Sixth Street in his apartment locked up and waiting for his mother. "Hey, Jordan, we're heading home," Jay said after the pickup game and Jordan would extricate himself from the playground structure and nearly run toward home. Lay always laughed at the idea of Jordan missing out on his opportunity to be with Jay. He didn't then know how to explain the feeling to Jay or Jordan. So, instead, he just smiled and laughed and kicked at Jordan or punched Jay, appreciated them both.

Lay never felt uneasy by Jay's side. Any other time, the walk from the park would have been tense. Big boys, corner boys, were always lurking. The walk from the park back to Jay's house was never rushed. Jay was always aware. He nodded to the corner boys. The corner boys nodded at Jay and Lay. They shook their heads at Jordan who was always making faces and sticking his tongue out at them.

Jordan like Lay liked dribbling the basketball and when he got bored Jay always lifted his chin toward Lay. Jordan thankfully gave the basketball to Lay.

Jay let Lay dribble the basketball all the way back and never protested in how long it took for Lay to dribble and walk.

"Hey, will you show me how to dribble better?"

"Sure," Jay said with a smile. "I can teach you both how to dribble better."

Once back on Twentieth and in the backyard, Jay showed Lay how to dribble with a little more control. The lesson did not take too long. Lay was surprised at the simplicity of the instruction. In a few minutes he was able to dribble through his legs and with either hand.

"That's pretty good," Jay said with a big grin on his square face.

"You think you could show me how to shoot?"

Jay twisted his lips on his face before answering. "Look, I ain't that kind of person," Jay said.

Lay raised his hands in surrender. "Come on, I promise to listen and not be a pain," Lay said as a matter of fact.

"Well, I was wondering if you could give me a refresher? I mean, I have the basics, but I want to dribble between my legs and behind my back," Lay said effortlessly.

"That's it?"

"Yeah, that's it," Lay said with a nod.

By the middle of the summer Lay could dribble and shoot pretty well. He wasn't the second coming, but he wasn't as horrible as he had been. The thing about playing and learning how to dribble and play basketball with Jay was similar to playing Monopoly with the family. There were strategies to it all.

Chapter 11. The video

Lay was dropped off on Twentieth for the day and after saying hello to everyone and finding Jay at work he went outside and up the block looking for Cass.

Cass's brother, Kenard was shirtless when Lay came by looking for Cass. The older brother had a bunch of tattoos on his arms and chest. There was a pistol, a skull, a panther and then a bunch of designs that looked like Chinese writing for some reason on his arms. Over his heart was a lion's head. On his stomach was a tattoo that read: Underwood. He was mean looking and had an earring and a thick gold chain around his neck. He was wearing boxer shorts, baggy jeans, a black leather belt and some white basketball sneakers.

"Cass ain't here," Kenard said.

"Is he coming back?"

"Not today," Kenard said. "He's with his... uncle."

Lay walked away from Cass's house and back toward Randolph and the end of the block looking for some of his friends. No one was around. He continued walking and was nearly at the end of the block when he ran into Eli and Reg on their bikes. Behind them came Darryl and Freddy.

"Hey, what happened to Cass?" Lay said as he reached out to slow Eli. Reg slowed too.

"What you mean?" Eli asked, looking at Lay curiously.

"Don't know," Lay said unsure. "He ain't around?"

"Yeah, he got in trouble," Darryl said stopping his bike and climbing off.

"What kind of trouble?"

"You didn't hear," Freddy said with a wide smile. "He got whooped."

"Whooped? By who?"

Eli and Reg looked at Freddy. Darryl shook his head. Eli and Reg were slow pedaling and stopped and climbed off their bikes and walked them with Lay. Behind them Freddy climbed off his bike as well.

For a long moment neither Eli nor Reg spoke.

"What happened?" Lay asked breaking the silence.

"Cass tried to steal something from Mar Mar from Nineteenth. You know Mar Mar and that crew don't play."

"Who's Mar Mar?"

"Avenue hard boy," Eli said. "They are always hanging out over by the liquor store on the corner."

"What did he steal?"

"Don't know. Just know that whatever it was Cass didn't deny it and that was enough to start the ass kicking," Reg said with a shake of his head.

"Damn," Lay said as they reached the middle of the block and his cousin's house. The four boys looked at the Beck house and then at Lay. Lay kept walking.

Lay, Reg and Eli kept walking toward their end of the block.

"Think Darryl got it on video," Eli said. Lay looked back.

Darryl nodded.

"Can I see it?"

"Let's stop at old man Harris's house," Darryl said. "He ain't home and there's shade over there."

They walked up Twentieth a few more houses and stopped in front of the house they deemed old man Harris's. It sat back off the street. There was a long walk to the dark brown brick prairie house. It was a quiet home.

"I like coming here during the day because, you know the rumor around the neighborhood is, Mister Harris is a vampire," Eli said.

"Of course, there was no solid evidence," Reg said with a grimace sitting on the lawn.

Lay looked at Eli and Reg and smiled. The two boys always acted so tough, Lay recalled, but then there were moments when they let slip their tough front and appeared as the eleven or twelve-year-old they were despite living in Underwood. They were filled with dreams, fantasies and unexplainable curiosity just like Lay or any other eleven or twelve-year-old.

"I don't know if old man Harris is a vampire," Freddy said. "I ain't seen him, but I'm leaning toward him being a ghoul."

"What's a ghoul," Lay said thinking he knew what a vampire was and a zombie, but his monster lore was kind of shaky after that.

"Well, according to the experts a ghoul is not truly a monster but a demon," Darryl said as he stopped in front of the house with the five trees on the yard. Two trees were close to the sidewalk. There were three more deeper on the property and closer to the house.

"The ghoul is a creature that eats the dead," Freddy said.

"The problem with old man Harris being a ghoul is that there is no graveyard near us," Reg said to Darryl and Freddy.

"Come on, there's a graveyard just behind Township East. So, if you are a ghoul, you are probably sleeping most of the day and at night you pop out and drive in your ghoulish car down to Township East and munch on some dead bodies," Freddy said.

"Hey," Eli said, stepping between Freddy and Darryl. "We came here to show Lay the video."

"Ain't no ghoul going to a graveyard behind a high school to eat," Reg said, trying to be the last word on ghouls.

"Reg, stop," Eli said, annoyed.

"Too easy to get caught," Reg concluded.

Lay felt like a basketball bouncing back and forth between the two camps. Vampires and ghouls. Lay smiled at Darryl and Freddy and shook his head at Reg and Eli. None of them was without monster and demon leanings.

Reg sulked. Freddy pouted. Eli shook his head.

"Yeah, just show him the video," Reg said with a frown.

In the shade of the two big trees Darryl sat on the manicured lawn and fished out his cell phone. Eli and Reg sat on the lawn sipping their sodas they bought at the corner gas station just a couple of blocks over. Freddy sat close to watch the fight. Lay sat next to Darryl and watched the video begin and instantly on the phone screen he could see a fight circle form just a few houses away.

"Cass messed with the wrong dude," someone said on the video.

"We can't get through a summer without at least one fight," a girl wearing a T-shirt and jeans said running by the camera.

"Well, this better be good," someone else said in the small crowd.

The video was shaky at first. People were bumping into Darryl as he recorded. There was a bunch of jostling.

Then Darryl found a place to record where no one bumped into him. There were easily ten or fifteen people circling the pair in the middle of the circle. In the middle of the circle stood Cass wearing a T-shirt, jeans and sneakers. The other person in the circle was Mar Mar.

Mar Mar was a high school tough with a diamond earring in his earlobe. He was not incredibly muscular, but he is not skinny in any way. He was shirtless and his long arms have ropy muscles. On his wrist was an expensive watch. Around his neck was a gold chain and a gold medallion of two numbers. He was wearing boxers and baggy black jeans. A black leather belt held up his jeans. On his feet were black and red basketball sneakers.

Lay watched and saw the familiar faces of Eli, Ricky, Dewey and Freddy in the circle. There was a bunch of screaming. People were waving and yelling and pushing.

Two people stood out in the circle. They were older, maybe high schoolers. Compared to most in the crowd the two looked like men. One even had a mustache.

One looked like Mar Mar except he was wearing a T-shirt. He stood in the crowd with sunglasses on and his arms crossed watching the fight.

The other boy, a milk dud colored boy, who had a mustache, had a tattoo on his hand and was wearing a reversed baseball cap and unbuttoned baseball jersey. He had a small face with intense eyes and a wide mouth. He was scowling at everyone, wearing black jeans and blue and orange basketball sneakers. He was wearing a gold chain and Lay saw the gold 19 medallion for Nineteenth Avenue.

The crowd was mostly neighborhood kids. In the crowd were Franky, Zeke and Huey, at least it looked like them. The inner circle, watching the fight was fifteen or so people. On the outer circle were other unfamiliar faces.

The cell phone camera angle changed. Cass and Mar Mar were circling each other. Mar Mar seemed so smug and confident. Cass swung at Mar Mar and Mar Mar ducked the punch easily.

Mar Mar let Cass try to hit him. He was toying with Cass. The older boy was laughing at Cass.

Cass, frustrated, ran at Mar Mar and the older boy waited until the absolute last moment before he sidestepped the charging Cass. Mar Mar stuck out his foot and tripped Cass and Cass went tumbling into the bushes.

"Okay, I'm bored humiliating you," Mar Mar said. Cass climbed back to his feet and turned ready to attack again. Mar Mar shook his head.

Mar Mar balled his fist and stepped forward and feigned a right jab and Cass ducked it only to come face-to-fist with the left. Mar Mar hit

Cass with a left-right combination which drove the younger fighter into the crowd of onlookers. The crowd caught Cass and threw him back at Mar Mar.

Mar Mar sidestepped Cass. Cass seemed drunk, in the video. He stumbled around looking for help. He tried to lift his hands and defend himself.

The bigger and older boy hit Cass in the stomach and all the air in Cass escaped him. He fell to his knees. Mar Mar walked around Cass and shook his head at the defenseless boy.

Mar Mar looked to the two in the crowd watching the fight. The one who looked a little like Mar Mar nodded. Mar Mar nodded as well.

"Little poo butt, you'll learn today," Mar Mar said. "You lucky I ain't murk you right here on this street corner."

Mar Mar grabbed Cass and dragged him to his feet. Cass tried to hit Mar Mar.

Mar Mar laughed at the feeble efforts by Cass. The high schooler stopped near the end of the fight and looked around the circle.

"If any of yous want more then bring it. I ain't scared. Tell your brother I ain't scared of his punk ass either. I'm Mar Mar. The Mar Mar. So nice they named me twice. Nineteenth Avenue Boy. Ain't nothing scare us."

Cass was bleeding from his mouth and nose. Mar Mar turned and saw Cass wobbling on shaking legs.

"You see all this? This is what happens when you think you something you not. Ain't nobody untouchable. Ain't nobody untouchable. You come for me and disrespect me, you get this and worse."

Mar Mar grabbed a handful of Cass's T-shirt and punched Cass so hard he crumbled on the sidewalk unmoving. Mar Mar stood and for an instant it looked like the older boy was thinking of doing something worse. But he walked away with his two thuggish friends.

"Damn," Lay said shocked.

"Yeah, damn," Darryl said.

"What's going to happen now?" Lay said to Darryl.

Darryl shrugged his shoulders as an answer.

Chapter 12. Don't get killed

One Thursday that summer Lay asked Hanna to call his mother to see if he could just spend the night. Hanna called. His mother said she didn't mind.

Jay got home from work and went to wash up and Lay's aunt served dinner to her children and Lay. They had chicken, mashed potatoes, corn on the cob, biscuits and a fresh Caesar salad. Jay, Jordan and his aunt drank juice. Lay and Hanna drank grape soda. While they were eating their father, Lay's uncle arrived home.

"Hey, everyone," Uncle Joe said, entering the house dressed in his work clothes. "Lay, is it Friday?"

Lay lowered his head at his uncle's ribbing. He poked Lay in the side playfully as he entered the kitchen and saw his nephew getting a glass of water. Lay smiled and scurried back to the kitchen counter across from Jay.

"Lay asked to stay over tonight," Aunt Bree said. "It's not a problem, is it?"

Uncle Joe shook his head. He smiled at everyone. As he walked out of the kitchen and headed to wash up, he hugged his wife and gave her a gentle kiss on the cheek. He put a hand on Jay's shoulder and patted Jordan on the head and blew a kiss to Hanna as he walked past the table.

In a few minutes he came back with his hands washed and face cleaner than it had been moments before. At his seat was a plate with chicken, potatoes, corn and biscuits. On the side was a small salad.

Uncle Joe sat down.

"What do you want to drink?" Aunt Bree asked.

"Mom, you sit down and eat," Jay said climbing to his feet. "Pops what you drinking?"

"Just water, Jay," his father smiled. "Thanks."

That night, at the dinner table Jordan got in trouble for playing with his food. Hanna smirked. She had warned him enough times. Jay sat and ate dressed in his light blue collared shirt he wore to the grocery store. His father, a thicker and rounder faced version of Jay, sat next to his mother and watched her every move.

Lay could not help but smile at the palatable love from Jay's parents. Jay's mother was an attractive woman in her prime of life. She and Hanna had the same pear shape.

After dinner the family watched a movie on cable. Jay talked to his father about a possible lead on his dream car. Lay listened and got tired. He fell asleep and woke up in the front room under covers.

That Friday morning Lay lounged around the Beck house watching TV and just not doing much. Everyone had their morning routine. Hanna's mother usually got up first. Lay, a light sleeper, usually woke with his aunt coming from the bathroom. He didn't usually climb off the couch until someone came into the living room. That Friday, no one came to the living room. So, the little round-faced son of Kimberly Payton just listened to the house awakening.

Hanna was the third person to wake and begin her day. She had a bedroom upstairs, in between her parents' bedroom and the bathroom upstairs. Hanna woke and immediately turned on her clock radio. She listened to a local R&B station that was always threatening to announce a winner of a contest. Jordan was the second to last to wake. Their father, Joe Beck, woke usually when he heard Hanna's radio, but rarely got out of bed until nine or ten. He worked two jobs and was always tired.

Jay was the last to climb out of bed and it was usually because of Jordan that he did get out of bed. Jordan loved waking up Jay. He would sing to him or scream at him or whatever annoying thing he could imagine snapping Jay awake.

Lay's Aunt Bree would make breakfast and the smell of eggs and bacon and toast brought everyone to the table. Jordan was all smiles and next to his mother in the morning to protect him from the annoyed Jay. Hanna was setting the table and Lay helped wherever he could. The six ate at the kitchen table and kitchen counter. Jay preferred the counter and as a result the kitchen counter was where Lay ate his breakfast. Jordan, Hanna, her mother and father ate at the kitchen table.

"Is your mom getting you tonight, Lay?" His uncle asked, sipping his coffee.

"Nope, I asked her if she would let me stay overnight last night," Lay smiled, chewing on his piece of buttered toast.

His uncle nodded.

"Well, what do you have planned for today?"

"I have to go to the grocery store this morning, should be there until two today," Jay said already dressed in his blue shirt and khaki pants.

"Well, I have to go see Verna," his aunt said.

"Hanna you're in charge," her mother said. "I should be back by one, at the latest. Boys you listen to Hanna while I'm away."

Everyone that Friday morning busied themselves. There was only one bathroom in the whole house. So, Hanna and her mother went to the bathroom first. They cleaned up and when they exited Jay and his father went into the bathroom. They cleaned up and when they exited Jordan went to the bathroom. Lay decided to wait. He was in no hurry. When he finally got into the bathroom, he brushed his teeth, washed up and changed into a fresh pair of clothes for the day.

When he exited the bathroom, the house seemed empty. His uncle was walking out of the backdoor and talking to Jordan.

"I have to go and get some equipment for the band," Uncle Joe said. "I have to check on some possible gigs before I go to work. So, you can't come with me. Need you to be a good boy and help your sister. Can you do that?"

Jordan nodded, dejected.

His aunt was already gone by the time Lay got out of the bathroom. Jay had left for work. There was just Hanna and Jordan in the kitchen when Lay returned from the front room dressed in his clean T-shirt, clean cut off jean shorts and sneakers.

"You need me to help you with anything?"

"You need me to help you with anything?" Jordan said, repeating what Lay had said, with a big smile.

"Well, Jordan could you put all the dishes in the sink?" Hanna said turning to Lay. "And can you sweep the kitchen?"

Cleaning the kitchen did not take long.

The Friday was extremely quiet. Lay played Connect Four with Jordan and Sorry with Hanna and Jordan before going to bed.

The Saturday after Lay saw the video of Mar Mar and Cass he walked outside and found Cass on the street. Lay hesitated. Then he figured Cass would be happy to see him.

Lay walked down to Cass and checked in on him.

"What's up?"

Cass looked a little beaten up still.

"Did your brother tell you I came by looking for you the other week?"

Cass nodded.

"Well, I was just checking on you," Lay said with a smile. He turned and walked away not sure what he expected.

He returned to the porch and looked down the street toward where Cass had been. Cass was gone. Maybe it was for the best, Lay thought. Cass had some things to figure out.

Lay turned and was about to go inside when he heard a basketball bouncing behind him. Lay turned toward the street and there was Cass dribbling his basketball. He smiled awkwardly.

"You want to go shoot some hoops?"

Like before the pair walked to the park.

Cass seemed to be smirking, Lay noticed.

"What's going on?"

"Nothing," Cass said.

"You sure?"

"Yeah, I'm sure," Cass said in a growl.

The pair walked slowly toward the park.

"Heard you go to that Catholic school in the east," Cass said with a sneer.

"Yeah, so," Lay said uncertain what Cass was aiming at.

"How you afford it?" He looked at Lay curiously. "It cost to go there, right?"

"I don't know, maybe, I guess," Lay said unsure of Cass's tone.

"How you not know?" Cass said angrily.

Lay stopped; they were just a block from the park. Cass stopped dribbling his basketball. He looked at Lay through menacing eyes.

"What's this?" Lay said to Cass trying to understand.

"What this is, is me trying to figure out if you are playing some kind of hustle game with me?" Cass said, venom in his words.

"A hustle game?" Lay asked, suddenly confused.

"Yeah, you trying to hustle me?"

"What?" Lay asked surprised by Cass's words.

"Yeah, my brother said some kids get bored and want to see how the other side lives and come down and hustle us and laugh at us later on," Cass said.

"I don't know what you're talking about," Lay said suddenly on guard. Cass seemed angry and dangerous.

Cass balled his fist and Lay took a step back.

"I ain't playing no hustle games. I don't even know what that is, and I just thought we were going to shoot hoops," Lay said studying Cass.

Cass took a step forward and Lay instinctively took another step back.

"Damn you," Cass said to himself. He seemed to be trying to make a decision. He hesitated.

Lay thought Cass was going to try and rush him and knock him to the ground. Instead, Cass walked away muttering something under his breath, clenching and unclenching his fists.

Lay watched Cass walk away. He looked down and noticed he had his hands balled into fists. He didn't know when he balled his fists or more importantly wasn't aware when he had prepared for Cass's attack. He watched as Cass walked angrily away.

Lay was unsure what to do. Was he supposed to run after Cass? Was he supposed to make sure things were okay between him and Cass? The eleven-year-old stood thinking and found he wanted to scream out of frustration.

He cautiously walked back toward Twentieth and was not sure if Cass wasn't going to turn around and attack him at any moment.

When Lay got back to Twentieth Street, he saw Cass walk to his house and enter. Cass lived on the eastside of Twentieth and his cousin's house was on the westside of the street. So, Lay walked on the opposite side of the street where Cass lived. When he got parallel to his friend's house he tried not to look. He made sure to keep the house and the front of the house in his periphery, just in case Cass decided to do a sneak attack.

When he finally reached the front of his cousin's house Lay was trembling. He looked back as he had been since passing the house where Cass lived, and Cass was walking down the street with his fists balled up and ready to fight. Lay did not run; he stood his ground.

"What's wrong with you?"

Cass did not answer with words. Instead, when he was in arm's reach, he swung with all his might at Lay's head. Lay backed up just in time as the punch missed his face. Cass threw another punch and hit Lay in the side. Instinctively, Lay threw out a punch and hit Cass in the ear. The punch from Cass was not punishing but it was surprising. Lay backed up and onto the front lawn of the Beck house. Cass took a step forward and again swung at Lay's face. This time Lay instinctively blocked the punch and pushed Cass back onto the sidewalk.

By Cass's next attack Hanna and Jordan were on the porch and Val, Eli, Darryl and Dewey were on the sidewalk watching and recording everything.

"What is going on?" Val said to Eli.

"Not too sure," Eli said focused on the fight.

"Think Cass thinks Lay is hustling us," Dewey and Darryl said over one another.

"What?"

"You know, like pretending and talking about us when he ain't here," Dewey said as an answer.

"What?"

"Why?" Eli said, suddenly confused.

"Hey, that's what he was telling us the other day," Darryl said holding his camera and recording the fight.

Cass threw another punch and Lay stepped back and the punch did nothing but blow past Lay's head. Lay moved to the right and then the left.

"Hit 'em," said Jordan.

Hanna looked at Jordan and despite Lay being in a fight smiled. She looked at the two boys on the front lawn and gritted her teeth.

"Lay, don't let him punk you," said Hanna from the porch.

"Don't let him punk you," Jordan said, repeating what Hanna said.

Cass stepped forward and grabbed Lay by his T-shirt and Lay instinctively pushed him away. Cass was surprised at Lay's resistance. Cass slid back. He composed himself and stepped forward and punched Lay as hard as he could in the stomach. The punch knocked the wind out of Lay and suddenly he was on his knees on the lawn. Cass reared back and threw a big punch at Lay's head.

The pain of the punch was nothing compared to the feeling of Cass's irrational thinking and betrayal for no apparent reason. Lay hit the ground and while on the ground Cass kicked him two or three times before Hanna and Jordan ran Cass off. Eli, Darryl and Dewey ran with Cass.

"Damn," Val said, the only person remaining when Hanna and Jordan picked their cousin up off the lawn.

Chapter 13. Training

"You okay?" Jordan asked Lay, unsure. He was still in his SpongeBob pajamas. On his feet were the house slipper heads of SpongeBob. Jordan helped Lay up off the front lawn. Lay looked up and saw Val standing there with her arms folded in front of her and her hip out. She looked like she was about to spit. Hanna was walking back to the front lawn, dressed in flip-flops, a skort and T-shirt.

"I don't know what that was, but I don't think it was a fight," Val said with a shake of her head.

"You okay?" Hanna asked Lay, concerned.

"He got a cut over his eye," Val said, pointing to the small cut above Lay's left eye.

"Yeah," Jordan said making a face.

"You need to clean that up," Val said. "Before it gets infected."

"Lathan Alexander don't lead with your face," Hanna said with a slight grin.

"You going to fight him again?" Val asked. "If you do, I think you might want to think about it. You are a lousy fighter."

"Val, go home," Hanna said annoyed.

"I was just trying to let him know that fighting ain't his talent," Val said confided.

"Val," Hanna said again a little louder.

"I'm leaving," Val said, spinning on her heels and walking across the street and toward her house.

Inside and away from prying eyes Hanna led Lay to the small bathroom with Jordan in tow. In the bathroom, Hanna told Jordan to get some cotton balls and Band-Aids. She looked for the Hydrogen Peroxide.

"This might hurt," Hanna said pouring some Hydrogen Peroxide on some cotton balls. "Close your eye. Don't let any of this get in your eye. It's not supposed to go in your eye."

Hanna pressed the cotton ball against Lay's cut and the pressure from Hanna against the cut was the only uncomfortable thing Lay felt.

"Jordan, give me a Band-Aid."

Lay kept his eyes closed as Hanna pressed a Band-Aid against his eyebrow.

With just Hanna and Jordan cleaning up Lay the inevitable questions came steadily.

"What was all that about?"

Lay did not respond.

"Lathan, what did you do to get Cass mad?"

"I didn't do anything," Lay said with his eyes closed.

"Come on, you had to do something," Hanna said looking at her cousin.

"Nope, we were going to the park to shoot hoops," Lay said and stopped. "Can I open my eyes?"

"Sure."

Lay looked in the mirror and there were all three of them captured there. Hanna with her short curly hair parted on the side of her diamond-shaped head in a T-shirt from some band. Jordan, with his round cheeks and bowling ball head dressed in his yellow SpongeBob pajamas shaking his head at Lay. Lay as he stood in the mirror looked a lot like his mother, milk chocolate colored, the distinct oval face with the high cheekbones and the sprinkling of freckles just visible beneath his brown skin that sprayed from cheek to cheek and across the bridge of his straight round nose. Beneath his nose Lay had full lips. Over his left eye Hanna had secured a Star Wars Band-Aid.

Lay shook his head upon seeing the Band-Aid.

Jordan grinned.

Hanna, all business, tapped Lay.

"You were saying," Hanna said trying to get Lay to speak.

"He said something about being hustled and then got mad and walked back home."

"That's it?"

"That's it," Lay said with a shrug of his shoulders.

"Cass is crazy," Jordan said, walking out of the bathroom.

Hanna pushed Lay out of the bathroom. Once out of the bathroom Lay started to think about what his mom or his aunt or uncle might say. He paused as Hanna walked past him and to the kitchen.

"You ain't going to tell anyone about what happened?"

Jordan looked at Lay from In front of the TV.

"Who wants to hear how you threw your face into Cass's fist," Jordan said laughing.

"No, I wasn't planning on saying anything," Hanna said to Lay.

"Yeah, and it will all blow over," Lay said hopefully.

Hanna looked at Jordan and back at Lay. Jordan twisted his lips trying to find the right words.

"Things like what we just saw don't blow over around here," Jordan said with a smirk.

"He's right," Hanna said agreeing with Jordan.

A week later and the next Saturday morning after the fight with Cass, over breakfast, his uncle sat at the table and shoveled in his food like a conveyor belt. Lay watched his uncle eat. It was incredible his consumption. When he finished his bacon, toast and scrambled eggs he sat and watched Lay curiously. He sipped at his coffee and studied his nephew. Lay noticed.

He lowered his head and ate his breakfast. There was no way Lay could hoover in the food like his uncle. So, he just at under the watchful eye of his mother's brother.

At the table that morning was his uncle and Jordan. Hanna had gone to something at school that Saturday morning with her mother. Jay was either sleeping or at work.

"Is Jay here?" Lay said to get his uncle to blink.

"No, he went to work," his uncle said.

"Dad," Jordan said, poking at his food aimlessly.

His father raised his index finger and Jordan fell silent.

"The world is about to get really hard for you. There are a bunch of people who aren't nice. They are bullies. Only way I know to deal with a bully is make him stop bullying you is standing up to him. Nine times out of ten that's enough. But sometimes, a bully is stubborn," his uncle said. "They need to realize there's a fight coming every time they want one," his uncle said.

Lay listened not sure how to respond.

"You know how to fight?"

"What?"

"You know how to fight?"

"You mean like Bruce Lee?"

His uncle grinned at Lay's response. "No, I mean, like to survive?"

Lay hesitated.

"Next Saturday I'll teach you how to handle yourself." He paused and looked at Lay. He added, "You and me have a date for training."

"Date? Training?"

"Yep," Uncle Joe said. "You'll thank me."

"Why?"

"I heard about you and that kid Cass," Uncle Joe said.

"That was nothing."

"Well, nothing has a way of becoming something around here and I ain't always going to be around."

Lay sat and listened.

"Everyone needs to know how to handle themselves, unless you expecting someone to save you."

Lay didn't respond. He was tired. He needed to lay down.

Uncle Joe, having finished his conversation with Lay, turned his attention to Jordan.

"Jordan, you finished eating?"

"Daddy, do I need to learn to fight?"

His father smiled. He looked at Jordan sitting at the kitchen table next to him and Lay suddenly quiet and sulking. Uncle Joe checked his watch. He paused. "Of course," his father said. "Finish eating. Both of you go clean up and put on some clothes and meet me out back in ten minutes." Uncle Joe looked around the kitchen and exhaled. He climbed to his feet and Lay did as well. Jordan still had food to eat, but he climbed to his feet as well.

"Okay, I'm going to clean up the kitchen and you both are going to brush your teeth, wash under those armpits and change into something comfortable and meet me out back."

With that Jordan was in motion. Lay followed his cousin downstairs only to reverse his direction and go to his backpack in the living room. He grabbed his toothbrush and went to brush his teeth.

True to his word Uncle Joe met his son and Lay in the backyard. He was dressed in a soiled work shirt, canvas trousers and his work boots. Uncle Joe was stretching when Jordan finally emerged from the backdoor of the house a few minutes after Lay.

"Now, before we begin let me tell you that no one in our family starts fights," Uncle Joe said. "We aren't bullies. But at the same time, we don't get pushed around. If someone wants to fight us, then we ain't running and we know how to end a fight."

"Daddy, does Hanna know how to fight?"

"Of course, I taught Jay and Hanna. It just makes sense to teach you and Lay," Uncle Joe said looking at the two boys in the backyard.

Lay stood on the concrete slab of the backyard where the wooden table sat and the bricked firepit. Hanging from the roof of the garage was a basketball rim.

"Okay, let me say that if you take what I teach you and become a bully I will sic Hanna on you to teach you a lesson," Uncle Joe said.

"Hanna wouldn't mess with me," Jordan said hopefully.

Uncle Joe chuckled at Jordan's confidence.

"Would she?"

Lay nodded his head in answer.

"Okay, down to business," Uncle Joe said. "In our world you ain't going to run into a lot of sophisticated fighting. They are just going to try and knock your block off. If they get in a few good hits, then they might get all crazy and then things will go bad."

"Bad?" Lay asked, curious.

Uncle Joe ignored Lay for the moment.

"Stand like this," Uncle Joe said. "If someone comes at you straight ahead you need to be ready to defend yourself."

For the next forty minutes Lay's uncle showed Jordan and Lay rudimentary moves. The moves were mostly defensive.

Lay stopped and looked at his uncle, curious.

"Why do I need to know how to fight?"

"You know where we are." Uncle Joe shook his head. "When I moved here, I lived in the city first. The city can be tough. You have to be tough to live in the city. I didn't want to raise a family in there. So, I moved to Underwood. Thought the suburbs were going to be better. It ain't. We don't live in a bad neighborhood, but the whites ran away. They leaving meant the cops ain't quick to respond. So, things ain't always going to be great. Ain't nobody giving nobody a pass around here. You walk down the wrong street in Underwood, and you smell weak, you'll find yourself in a fight."

"I don't want to live like that," Lay said defiantly.

"I don't want to live that way either, but as far as I can tell you look like me and I look like you and we didn't take no magic pill that says lay off us because we're special. So, we got to make sure anyone that steps to us knows we ain't soft or going easy."

Lay shook his head.

"It's to make sure we are safe," Jordan said, paying attention to his father.

"Right," Uncle Joe said.

Lay fell silent.

"It's our insurance," Jordan said with a smile. "Jay said that before."

They continued practicing for the inevitable. After a few minutes of practice Lay stopped.

"Uncle Joe you a fighter?"

"I wouldn't say I'm a fighter. I did some boxing when I was a kid. I know how to fight. But would not say I'm a fighter. I would say that if someone starts something with me, I know how to end the fight quickly."

"How?"

"Practice and patience," Uncle Joe said to Lay. "Most fights don't last long. They are all energy and anger, and they wear themselves out after a couple of minutes. If you know what you're doing and weather that first storm you can shut down things pretty quickly."

Lay nodded.

Jordan and Lay listened to Uncle Joe's instructions. Lay could not believe how different Jordan was when his father gave him directions. He didn't grouse. He didn't question. He just did what he was told with a smile on his face.

"You are doing well," Uncle Joe said sitting on the wooden tabletop. "I'm really impressed with both of you. You going to teach somebody a lesson if they ever come looking for trouble."

Jordan continued to practice his move. Lay seemed a little more reflective.

"Here's a tip. Most people go for the head, trying to knock someone out. The stomach is more important. You hit the chin and you could break your hand. You kill the stomach, and you kill the head."

Lay and Jordan listened.

"Okay, back to work," Uncle Joe said. "You need to practice this stuff every day until you can do it in your sleep." He paused. "I'm trying to make sure you two stick around for a few years," his uncle said, with a broad smile.

Lay looked at his uncle curiously.

"What do you mean?"

"People fight for all sorts of reason. What I am teaching you is to protect you and if anyone steps to you then you can pull it out and say, back up or you 'bout to taste your lunch," his uncle said.

"Taste your lunch," Jordan said, with a chuckle.

"Yeah, taste your lunch," Uncle Joe said with a hearty chuckle.

The three worked diligently. Jordan was a great student under the tutelage of his father. Lay was apt. He wanted to know why they did things rather than just doing things.

Near the end of the training uncle showed them a strange move. Jordan tried the move. Lay tried it as well.

"No, like this," his uncle said. His uncle bent his knees and threw out a lightning right hand punch at the imaginary person in front of him.

Jordan seeing his father's deft move repeated the same move. Lay mirrored what he had seen his uncle do.

"That's good."

"Okay, now if someone comes up behind you," his uncle said. He flicked the hands off his shoulders and spun around and used the same deft movement to punch the invisible person. Lay and Jordan imitated their uncle and father.

Lay and Jordan were great students. They took to the training with his uncle and Uncle Joe was impressed with their improvement. Lay did not really think he was improving. It was just practicing simple moves and guessing sometimes what might happen and doing pushups and sit-ups.

Chapter 14. The last Monopoly game

Sometime after the neighborhood fireworks show Lay and Cass met up again. It wasn't like the last time, but there was still a tension there. The meeting happened a couple of weeks after the national fireworks. Lay returned to Twentieth and slept over and woke up to find that Jay had gone to work. Bored, he asked Jordan if he wanted to go to the park. Of course, Jordan did. So, Jordan and Lay walked to the park.

They were walking down Oak Street toward the park when Lay and Jordan saw Cass and Ricky near the park. Their bikes were on the grass. They had a kid, not much older than Jordan, up against a fence. Ricky looked like he was about to hit the kid when Lay and Jordan walked up.

A block away from the park and Lay saw a disturbing picture of Ricky and Cass bracing a kid with a tight fade who couldn't have been ten years old. Ricky stood with his fist balled up and ready to punch the round-faced boy wearing a green T-shirt and blue jeans. Cass was holding a handful of the boy's shirt in his hand as Lay pulled up to see Cass deliver a punch to the round boy's belly. The little boy crumpled in front of Cass. Ricky smiled. Cass smiled as well.

"What's going on?"

Cass turned and smiled, seeing it was Lay.

"If it ain't the pretender," Cass said with a sneer. "Don't step into this pretender. You hear me, Lay?"

Ricky held the kid by the front of his twisted T-shirt as Cass turned and studied Lay and Jordan.

"Pay attention to that punk," Cass said, looking at Ricky and then back to Lay and Jordan.

Ricky nodded and sneered, never taking his eyes of the little boy.

Jordan pushed Lay and he cut his dark eyes to his younger cousin.

"We should go," Jordan said.

"Listen to your little cousin, pretender," Cass said with a mirthless smile. "You don't want any of this."

Lay looked from Cass and to Jordan.

"Stay right here," Lay said to Jordan as he walked slowly and deliberately toward the two bullies. The nameless boy was on his knees holding his stomach and trying to catch his breath. The round boy placed a thick hand on the sidewalk and tried to climb to his feet.

"Don't forget what my dad taught us," Jordan said under his breath kicking out his leg and taking a fighting stance.

Lay looked back and Jordan got into a fighting stance like his father had instructed. Lay nodded and turned back to the two boys bullying the little boy.

Ricky cut his dark eyes from the boy trying to catch his breath back toward Lay as he got closer.

"Easy, Ricky," Lay said and noticed Cass was balling his fist as if to either fight Lay or hit the boy still struggling on the sidewalk.

In a few steps Lay was by Ricky. Cass was surprised to find Lay so close. Cass looked at the boy, Jordan and Ricky and without warning Lay, without thinking, stepped between Cass and the boy.

"What are you doing Cass?"

"Pretender, you don't want to step in between me and this, right now."

Lay had his hands up in front of Cass. Ricky stepped forward. Lay took a step back and made sure the boy was between him and the two boys.

"Cass, be careful," Lay said calmly.

"What I got to be careful about pretender?" Cass said with a smirk.

Lay looked at Cass and watched Ricky out of the corner of his eye.

"This ain't right, Cass. I don't know if you're right or not, but I know bad starts with the little things," Lay said evenly. He was watching as Ricky balled his fist. Lay expected Ricky to try something.

"What you think? I'm all of a sudden, the bad guy? That kid deserved it. He was talking smack to me and Ricky."

The boy climbed to his feet.

Ricky and Cass stood in front of Lay. Lay gestured to the little boy to leave. The boy stumbled away and after a few feet he turned.

"I'm going to tell my brother," the boy said tears in his words.

Lay looked back and the boy was running for the alleyway which separated the park from the other side of the block.

Ricky looked at Cass. Cass looked at Ricky. Lay put his hands up to stop the two if he had to that moment.

"What? You gonna chase him down?"

Ricky looked at Lay like he wanted to punch him. Cass smiled and nodded.

Ricky threw a looping punch at Lay. Lay was expecting the attack and was not surprised. What surprised him was how predictable the attack was, just like his uncle had told him weeks before.

Lay stepped out of the arc of the punch and waited for Ricky's second furious attack. He came at Lay all anger and fury. He swung at Lay and Lay dodged the left hook. Ricky threw an overhand right and Lay avoided that. Ricky paused and that was when Lay stepped forward and fired two hard punches into Ricky's midsection. The shots hit like bombs and Ricky fell to the ground, unable to breath. He knelt on the sidewalk trying to catch his breath.

Kill the stomach to kill the head, his uncle said.

Ricky reached out a big paw with his head down and looked like he was about to throw up.

Lay spun away from Ricky and turned to look at Cass. Cass was fuming.

"What? You learn how to fight?"

Cass studied Lay evenly. Lay looked at Ricky out of the corner of his eye. He found it interesting that Ricky was now on the sidewalk like the little boy before Lay showed up.

"That kid was just some little kid popping off," Lay said looking at the sneering Cass and checking the wheezing Ricky.

"You--," Ricky whined.

"You don't know how it works here pretender," Cass said, with a snarl. "We can't let little punks get away with disrespecting us. One disrespect leads to a hundred disrespects and then what do you have?"

"Chaos," Ricky exhaled through closed eyes.

Lay shook his head, suddenly frustrated.

"That kid wasn't as big as Jordan," Lay said trying again.

"What's that mean?" Cass scoffed.

Lay changed direction.

"This ain't you, Cass. You still like baseball? Or are you too tough for baseball and baseball cards?"

"I ain't got time for those kid games no more. Things are changing."

"Yeah, I bet," Lay said disappointed. "You listening to the wrong people. What they doing that is so special?" Lay paused, thinking. "I mean, I ain't no pretender but you let someone tell you I'm hustling you. You talked to me. We hung out." He stopped himself. "You know me."

"I ain't trying to hear this," Cass said, looking to Ricky and then Lay.

"I know you know me," Lay said imploring Cass.

Cass shook his head. Ricky climbed to his feet and took a deep breath.

"You lucky... we don't stomp you out... right now," Ricky said trying to catch his breath.

Lay looked at Ricky and thought about hitting him again. *Sometimes, a bully is stubborn*, his uncle said. They need to realize there's a fight every time they want one.

"Ricky, you stubborn?"

Ricky looked at Cass and then at Lay and turned away only to swing at Lay again. Lay saw the sneak attack coming and moved under the punch and hit Ricky once again in his soft midsection, dropping him again on the sidewalk.

Ricky shook his head on the sidewalk. He was trying to catch his breath.

Cass stepped forward and Lay turned to watch Cass.

"You can't sucker punch my friend and get away with it," Cass said.

"I didn't sucker punch no one," Lay said with a sneer. "He's tried to hit me twice. It's not my fault he's bad at this."

Cass and Lay stared at each other. Lay studied Cass, standing in front of him wearing a T-shirt, jeans and sneakers. He had his hand in his front jean pocket. He had that look on his face the time he and Lay had been on this same street and he started acting crazy.

"Not everyone starts out being the bad guy," Lay said easily. "I mean, most people would tell you they ain't bad. Right?"

"What you talking about?"

"I'm saying that something, someone, makes them bad. I just think it's the little things that push them and suddenly they are... bad."

Lay and Cass looked at each other. Cass stared intently at Lay.

"You thinking you better than us?"

Lay blinked at the words.

"No," Lay said discouraged. "I think you being told things that ain't true. You don't need to fight me."

"Oh, I think I do need to fight you," Cass said with an evil smile. He tapped his jean pocket front. Lay looked at the pocket not knowing what was hidden there. He shook Cass tapping his pocket from his mind.

"For what?"

"What?"

"Tell me what we fighting about," Lay said knowing that Cass really did not have a reason.

Cass opened and closed his mouth.

"See," Lay said with a little hope. He looked at Ricky still on his knees, who was the wildcard. Lay stared at Ricky and dared him to attack him. Ricky tried to climb to his feet again holding his stomach and deciding if he wanted to face the new Lay.

"We ain't bad," Lay said explaining. "We just put in bad situations. We lucky to survive, my uncle says," Lay said more to himself than to Cass or Ricky. He looked back and saw Jordan standing ready to fight. He smiled. "We got to make good decisions, or we turn out bad," Lay said to Ricky.

"I don't want to hear anymore from you. You better fly away," Cass said not as angry as he had been. "I'm going to show you I ain't the bad guy today. But the next time you get in my way I ain't gonna be so nice."

"Yeah," Ricky wheezed finally standing near Cass.

Lay nodded and backed up and he and Jordan walked to the park.

That was the last time Lay spoke to Cass in any significant way.

*   *   *

The following week the unofficial last Monopoly game of the summer was the week before Lay participated in his first Chase.

He didn't know that at the time. But things all had a way of working out for Lay.

The last time everyone played Monopoly that summer Hanna was the banker, and her father was in charge of the real estate cards as usual.

Hanna was the thimble. Lay's aunt was the old shoe. Lay's uncle was the top hat. Jay picked the racecar. Jordan was playing as the man on the horse. Lay usually ended up playing with the dog token.

Hanna and her father went over the rules.

"No one can buy property until they go around the board once," Hanna announced.

"Put five hundred on Free Parking," Hanna's mother said. Hanna, the banker nodded and placed an orange five-hundred-dollar bill in the center of the board.

"Every time we pass Go, we get two hundred dollars," Jay said to Lay.

"Every time we all pass Free Parking, we toss another one hundred in the kitty," Hanna's father said.

"That's it," Hanna said with a grin.

"One last thing," Hanna's father said, with a smile. "Everyone has to build property equally. You can't have a house on one piece of property and a hotel on the other."

While the pair gave instructions, Jay grinned at Lay.

"Why you grinning at me?"

"Jordan told me you taught Cass and Ricky a lesson," Jay said with a grin.

"Yeah, I heard you didn't let that bully get away with anything," Aunt Bree said with a smile.

"Good for you, Lathan," Hanna said with a slight grin.

Uncle Joe only smiled at Lay. Lay felt embarrassed. He gave Jordan a side glance.

"What? What did you expect? You know I like spilling the tea," Jordan said with a smile.

Lay shrugged off the attention and tried to concentrate on the Monopoly game. The third and last time the Beck's played Monopoly that summer Jordan quit after going around the board twice and getting frustrated that he could not play with the pieces on the board. He was uninterested in the rules and eventually drifted off the to the couch and TV. He fell asleep watching Madea.

With Jordan on the couch and watching Madea the last Monopoly game of the summer began in earnest and in five circuits around the board Lay had two properties on each side of the board. He had Mediterranean Avenue, Reading Railroad, Connecticut Avenue, St. Charles Place, New York Avenue, Illinois Avenue and Vermont Avenue. Somehow, he had scooped up Pacific Avenue on the most expensive side of the board but been unable to capture either Park Place or Boardwalk. He seemed to be cash poor to his cousins and aunt and uncle. Yet, as he made his way around the board, he avoided traps laid by the others.

"You want to sell anything?"

He did not look to his aunt or uncle. He simply rolled the dice and played.

The next time around Lay purchased the B&O Railroad from the bank and moved methodically around the board.

"You might want to sell me one of your properties," Hanna said as Lay passed Go and collected two hundred dollars. He looked down and noted his stash of money was decent, but nothing like his uncle's or Hanna's. With a quick glance it seemed Uncle Joe had the most money and then it was Hanna, Jay and maybe Lay and then his aunt. Lay did not concern himself with the money that early in the game.

His cousins and uncle were suddenly negotiating with Lay. They all thought he was in trouble. Everyone was giving the youngest player in the game advice.

Lay did not listen. Lay simply smiled at the players.

"Well, the game is going to get harder now," his uncle said, pointing out all the real estate was sold and now negotiations would be the next step toward monopolies.

"Lay, do you want to sell any property?" Hanna said with a big smile.

"No," Lay said with a bigger smile.

"Come on Lay, sell me Illinois Avenue and I will give you Oriental Avenue," said Jay, bargaining.

"That's not a good deal," his aunt said.

"Why?"

"Oriental is low-rent," his aunt said, scanning the board for properties. "Illinois is high-rent."

Lay smiled.

With all the property sold Lay checked the time and realized it was still relatively early. He knew if he could hold off the bargaining, he could stop most monopolies and with desperation prices for properties would rise.

"Lay, come on sell me one of your properties," Hanna said holding up Tennesse and St. James Avenue.

Lay shook his head no.

"He's playing hardball," Uncle Joe said with a smile. "He's learned how to play the game and he ain't going to be no pushover."

"He's slowing up the game," said Jay, angrily.

Lay looked at Jay confused.

"Don't be like that Jay, you know once you figure out things, everyone got to go their own way," Uncle Joe said, looking at Lay with a slight grin.

"So, you want to sell anything?"

"Nope," Lay said smugly.

The game continued and suddenly everyone was trying to get a monopoly that did not include Lay, but that was nearly impossible. Uncle Joe had landed on Park Place and bought it. Hanna owned Board Walk and she was not going to give it up in a tight game.

So, every turn, every player bargained with someone trying to sweeten the pot as tokens circled the board. Lay checked the clock and realized he had complete control of the game if he didn't cave in.

His aunt offered to buy Vermont Avenue in exchange for Virginia and St. James Avenue. The offer was tempting to the eleven-year-old. He hesitated and everyone at the kitchen table saw what seemed of interest to Lay.

"Wait, Lay, I'll give you Vermont and Connecticut for Illinois Avenue," Jay said to Lay.

"Okay, I'm going to break this game open," said Uncle Joe. "Lay, I'm going to give you five hundred dollars for Mediterranean. It's a great deal. You would be crazy not to take it. It's a low-rent piece of property. No one gets hurt with me owning that."

Lay sold his uncle Mediterranean, and it was surprisingly the property exchange that was the beginning of the end of the game. In two circuits Uncle Joe had his first hotels on the properties. He methodically negotiated with his wife and son and daughter and was the solitary owner of a monopoly.

When the clock struck ten o'clock Lay started to tire. Ten minutes later he sold Jay Illinois and the game became a fight for monopolies. He sold Vermont Avenue to his aunt. The last deal he made with Hanna before he surrendered.

"Hanna, I will sell you New York Avenue," Lay said confidently.

He climbed up from the table and walked away as the cutthroat game of Monopoly got underway. Lay could only smile at his handiwork. He had controlled the game until he tired. He had not lost. He had become sleepy. To win, Lay decided, he had to have all his wits about him.

That Monopoly game was in his head when Cass and Ricky talked about things changing.

Chapter 15. Skittles or Starbursts

Twentieth was split down the middle by the stupidest thing, Skittles. On one side of the block there were the Skittles Crew, which was made up of Cass, Greg, Tamra, Eli, Ricky, Rayshon, Darryl and Tobias. On the other side were the Starburst Crew led by Zeke and followed by Lay, Val, Darius, Reg, Franky and Huey. Even though the crews were led by Cass and Zeke the real power struggle fell to Cass and Lay.

Everyone on Twentieth saw the rift forming and were powerless to stop it. Some tried and failed. Some did not want to stop it.

Another week went by and when Lay walked out of his cousin's house Zeke was walking up the street. Seeing Lay, Zeke paused.

"What you doing?"

"Nothing," Lay said bored.

"Going to see what everyone is doing up the street," Zeke said. "Want to come?"

"Sure," Lay said jumping off the porch and catching up with Zeke.

"Heard about you and Cass," Zeke said, in no hurry.

"That's over," Lay said hopeful.

"Not what I heard."

"What'd you hear?"

"I heard after Cass tried to knock you out your cousin jumped in and stopped him from doing the do on you. He chalked it up to Hanna's loyalty," Zeke said with a little enthusiasm. "But the problem is that you overstepped and got in between him and Ricky checking some poo butt who was being disrespectful."

"The kid was like in third grade," Lay said with a shake of his head.

"Maybe, but Cass is talking about it and you ain't got your cousin to back you up," Zeke said.

"My cousin didn't do much," Lay said slightly annoyed.

"Not what I heard," Zeke said with a shrug of his shoulders. He slowed and added, "They ain't gonna do nothing with everyone around. Just hang back and things should be cool."

"I'm not worried about Cass or Ricky."

"You should be," Zeke said. "There's a lot of talk on the block."

"Was it coming from," Lay tried to remember who was at the fight. He continued, "Val? Eli? Darryl? Or Dewey?"

"Darryl had a video," Zeke said. "I didn't see it."

Lay nodded.

The two walked to the end of the block and found a handful of kids Lay had been friends with before the fight with Cass and Ricky. Zeke slowed.

"You don't have to come," Zeke said.

"No, we're cool," Lay said not sure if they were cool or not.

Zeke shrugged his shoulders and walked up to the loose knot of kids sitting in the shade of the trees on the lawn of old man Harris. Lay took a deep breath and as he approached counted all the friends he had before the fight and after the fight. After the fight he was sure of Zeke, Val, Darius, Reg, Huey and Franky. Everyone else was aligned with Cass and Ricky. Lay noticed a kid he had only seen a few times. Greg, Lay remembered. He lived on the other side of Oak Street.

Cass was sitting with his back against the tree, and everyone was circled up around him. He had a brown handled pocketknife in his hand when Lay showed up. Greg, the kite faced kid dressed in a T-shirt, cutoff jean shorts and sneakers, was sitting on his butt looking at Cass playing with his knife. Eli was lying on the grass with his knees up, in the half circle near Cass. Dewey, lying on his stomach, was watching Cass try to throw the knife into the grass point down. Also there on the grass was Darius, Franky and Huey.

Cass lifted the knife up in the air by the blade and threw it with a flick of the wrist into the grass, where it dug into the dirt blade down and handle up. He reached out and pulled the knife out of the dirt.

Rayshon, Darryl and Ricky were sitting on the curb. Rayshon and Darryl were kicking rocks at each other. Ricky was picking at a scab on his elbow. When Lay walked up Ricky immediately climbed to his feet.

Ricky balled his fists ready to fight. Lay looked at Ricky and tried to understand what the big chucklehead expected to happen. Lay did not blink.

Cass seeing Ricky bristle looked and saw Zeke and Lay standing on the sidewalk.

"If it ain't the leader of the Starburst crew and the pretender," Cass said with a smirk, grabbing his knife from the grass and standing.

Cass standing got everyone's attention and suddenly Eli was standing beside Dewey. Rayshon and Darryl were standing as well.

Darius, Franky and Huey climbed to their feet and moved toward Zeke.

"I didn't bring him down here to cause a problem," Zeke said.

"Well, you don't have to bring him to cause a problem," Cass said mockingly. "He is a problem."

Ricky stood near Darryl. Lay watched the tension crackle between the two groups.

"Look, I just was coming to see what was going on, nothing else. I ain't got time for silly stuff," Lay said suddenly annoyed. "I wanted to go shoot some hoops or do something rather than--."

"You suddenly in charge?" Cass said cutting Lay off.

Lay stared at Cass.

"You heard me," Cass said. "You think you in charge?"

"I ain't in charge," Lay said calmly.

"That's right," Cass said. "You don't even live on this block, pretender," Cass said with a sneer.

Lay looked at Zeke and shook his head.

"I'll be at my cousin's," Lay said frustrated and turned to leave. Zeke reached out and grabbed Lay's arm. Lay turned around.

"Don't leave," Zeke said. "Don't nobody have the right to run you off."

Darius and Franky were near Zeke and the two boys nodded in agreement.

"We got just as much right to be here as anybody," said Huey with a nod.

Eli was staring daggers at Darius.

"You know this summer is nearly over," Cass said. "Think we need to do something special for this last big summer."

"What you mean?" Eli said. "Last big summer?"

"This is probably the last summer we get to do kid stuff," Cass said.

"Yeah," Ricky said. He was tall for his age and thickly built. Lay looked at Ricky and tried to imagine he was eleven or twelve, but knew he was easily twelve or thirteen. "Time to move on from the kiddy stuff."

"Why?"

"We getting older," Cass said. "We got to grow up and move on from the games we been playing."

"Are there other games?" Asked Dewey.

Cass shrugged his shoulders in response.

"We ain't going to be kids forever," Ricky said.

"I don't want to give up on the things we like," Darryl said, his voice a little strained.

"Tough," Ricky said.

"Things are already changing," Cass said. "All your cuteness that was adorable a year ago is about to come to an end."

Everyone in ear shot stopped. Huey stood there like he was frozen.

"What are you talking about?" Darius asked.

"We all about to turn twelve and when we turn twelve, we go from cute to being seen as... no longer cute. We become just like everyone else," Cass said. "We ain't going to get... the benefit of the doubt next year. So, we got to get ready."

"Cass, that ain't true," Zeke said.

"It is," Ricky said. "As soon as school starts, they going to look at you different. They going to get upset quicker with you. They going to send you to the office faster. Just watch and see."

"What you saying?" Huey asked.

"Yeah, I don't believe that," Zeke said.

"Well, we ain't going to have the chance of being a non-threat the quicker we fill out," Cass said. "My brother told me to watch my back. This summer we go from cute to dangerous."

Lay and Huey shook their heads, unbelieving.

"You ain't got to believe me. Ask your brother or your cousin, he knows. Ask your uncle. He'll tell you if he still remembers being our age."

Cass smirked at everyone around him.

"Y'all just a bunch of kids playing kid games," Cass said. "The real world is going to eat you up and spit you out."

"The real world is all about power and money," Ricky said.

"The sooner you start to realize that the sooner you will start to figure out things," Cass said.

"How you know?" Asked Zeke. "I mean, you ain't grown."

Cass smiled. "You see this knife? My brother gave it to me. This is the first step into the real world. Everyone in the real world got a weapon." He sneered. No one challenged Cass or his statement. He continued. "In the real world no one cares about games. All they care about is money and power and nothing else."

"How you know?" Asked Franky, curious.

"My brother told me."

"Your brother don't work," Zeke said.

"My brother figured out the real world. He told me that in the real world there are those that work, like my mom and dad or your mom and dad or whatever. They are the squares. They are the... cogs, he said, in the machine," Cass said. "They working to live. Well, the rich and powerful are at the top of the machine pulling the strings and holding all the power."

"It don't make any sense," Darius said, confused.

"Where is your brother in the machine?" Asked Huey, curious.

"Okay, so my brother said that there are the squares, the cogs of the machine. They are inside the machine working away and getting nowhere. They are like those gerbils on that spinning wheel. You know?"

"Where's your brother? Is he making money?"

"My brother is on the outside of the real world. He is the dark side, the invisible side of the real world. He is doing whatever to gain power and money," Cass said, as an explanation.

"Doing whatever?"

"So, your brother will steal and rob to get power?" Asked Zeke, concerned.

Cass did not answer.

"Will he hurt someone to get power and money?" Lay asked, determined.

Cass looked and smiled at Lay.

"The real world is going to eat you up," Cass said, fiendishly.

"You believe someone who is going to do whatever to get money and power?" Lay asked. He shook his head and continued. "You already said he will lie, cheat and steal? And that's someone you trust?"

Chapter 16. Sundown

Late July the following week before August arrived Zeke, Val, Reg, Darius, Huey, Lay, and Franky sat on Eli's open porch and negotiated with Cass, Ricky, Eli, Darryl, Dewey and Rayshon. It was a monumental meeting. It was for bragging rights and street cred on Twentieth.

Zeke and Cass were the main negotiators. They had decided to have one last Chase and this Chase was going to shut up all the sniping going on back and forth between the two camps. At the end of the night there would be one winner and one loser. The winning camp would rule Twentieth until someone else other than the Skittles or Starburst group appeared.

Zeke bet comics. Each member of the Starburst crew brought one of their comics for the ante. Zeke brought his Black Panther series. Val brought her Watchman #1 sealed and boarded. Reg had a signed copy of The Sandman #7 sealed in a plastic bag he got from a comic book convention a few years ago. Darius had offered his Captain America #300. Huey offered up his X-Force #1 signed by Todd McFarlane. Lay gave his Batman Damned with the Batweenie issue for the Starburst crew. Franky had his unopened Death of Superman comic for the kitty. They were carefully packed in Zeke's backpack and after Cass agreed with them zipped up and prepared to be taken to the Stewart sisters.

Cass bet baseball cards. Cass brought his Negro League baseball collection. Ricky brought his Aaron Judge Rookie card. Eli brought 2020

Seven Pack Blaster Box. Darryl had an MLB Baseball Tin Trading Card collection. Dewey had a Ken Griffey Jr. Rookie card. Rayshon brought his prized Chrome Fernando Tatis Jr. Rookie card for the Skittles ante. The baseball cards were carefully packed in a baby-sized shoebox and packed into a backpack by Cass after Zeke agreed.

In the end, whichever crew won, the other crew lost and had to endure the memory of the last summer before they became teenagers as losers.

"So, we take these to the Stewart sisters, and they hold them until the end of the game," Cass said.

Zeke agreed.

The two groups walked from Eli's house to the house which sat on the southside of the street and just four doors away from the corner of Randolph Street.

Regine and Page Stewart were neighborhood legends. They lived in the Stewart house, which had been their home for three generations. It was one of those houses with a lawn in the front, a walkway and a long swath of grass which led to the backyard. The porch was big and bright and held a rocking lounger and a couple of chairs.

Everyone was afraid of the two dark sisters who nearly went to jail the year before for beating a girl half to death for threatening to take Page's boyfriend. No one dared threaten the Stewart sisters. Page was the fighter. Regine the mouth.

"Remember, we holding your crap until fifteen after nine tonight. Every minute past that is an extra dollar," Page said, evilly. Regine smiled and nodded.

"Cool," Zeke said. He was a long faced brown boy with thick eyebrows, almond shaped eyes, a broad nose and full lips. Zeke had wide shoulders for his age underneath his cartoon T-shirt. He was V-shaped with a thin waist that barely held up his oversized shorts and long muscular legs that ended in thick tube socks and basketball sneakers. Next to him, on the porch, was Lay, compact and dressed in a striped T-shirt, jeans and tennis shoes. Lay gave Regine five one-dollar bills.

Regine was holding Zeke's blue JanSport backpack. Inside sat the collection of comics from the Starburst's group. The collection of comics were the collective Starburst's pride and joy.

Cass, the square faced boy, smiled and gave Page his sealed baby shoebox and her money. He smiled a crooked smile and cut his dark eyes toward Zeke and Lay. He looked back to the street and saw Ricky and Darryl waiting on the sidewalk next to his bike.

Page was holding the rectangular shoebox which might have been a brick but was now home to the collection of baseball cards from Cass's group. The baseball cards were the Skittles' groups greatest treasure. They had spent all year trading and buying and trading to get them.

"No one messes with my stuff," Zeke said.

Regine nodded.

Cass looked at Page.

"You know ain't nobody stupid enough to come up on this porch and try and take something from us," Page said with a sneer.

As the Saturday sun began to set Regine and Page were enlisted by Zeke and Cass to be the bankers of a backpack and baby shoebox filled with baseball cards. Now, as bankers, Regine and Page Stewart did not care what was in the backpack Zeke gave her. They did not care what was in the baby shoebox. They did not know they were holding the comic and card collections. All they cared about was being paid to watch a backpack and a shoebox.

Zeke, Lay and Cass walked down the stairs of the Stewart girls house and back to the sidewalk. Darryl and Ricky seeing Cass coming picked up his black and gold BMX bike and awaited Cass's arrival.

"We good?" Lay asked looking at Cass once off the porch and headed toward the sidewalk.

"Naw, never, drop by," Cass said grabbing his bike and climbing on and Darryl and Ricky riding away from the Stewart house and toward the Oak Street end of the block where his crew were gathered doing bike tricks. Cass pulled back on his handlebars and rode half the way up the block doing a wheelie to his friends.

Zeke and Lay walked up the street toward old man Johnson's house where the Skittles group were gathered.

Old man Johnson's house was a big blue and white Victorian house like the apartment house next to Jay's house. There were half a dozen old Victorian houses on Twentieth.

"Tried to tell you nothing ends on Twentieth," Zeke said.

"Yep," Lay said with a shake of his head.

"How do you think it ends?"

"Don't know, really," Lay said with a shake of his head. "Guess we going to move in different directions."

The pair arrived back at the unofficial gathering spot for the Starburst group, the Alexander house. Sitting on the sidewalk were Val,

Darius, Reg, Franky and Huey. When Zeke arrived, Huey climbed to his feet. He seemed a little anxious.

"Man, Zeke, I think I want my comics back," Huey said.

"What?"

"I want my comic back," Huey repeated.

"Nope, no can do," Zeke said. "The Stewart sisters have the bet, and you are more than welcome to go and try and get your stuff but know they ain't giving out nothing but hard times and hurt feelings until nine fifteen tonight."

"It ain't fair," Huey said, complaining.

"Fair or not we all got something to win and something to lose tonight," Zeke said.

Old man Johnson's house sat in the middle of the block between Mister Alexander's house and Missus Chapel's house.

A little before sundown Cass and his crew climbed onto their bikes in front of the apartment house where they had been resting. The seven bikers behind Cass were dressed in T-shirts, jeans and tennis shoes. There was only one biker wearing shorts.

They slowly gathered at the corner. They popped wheelies and jumped on and off curbs. Cass gestured and they slowly rode to the middle of the block. Waiting there, between the Johnson's house and the Chapel's house, the two groups stared down each other.

"Here are da' rules. You's got 'til seven to run and hide. Y'all know the borders. Three blocks in any direction. No more. No one goes to Mexico City. So's that's us on Twentieth both sides and down to Saint Charles and back up to Oak. Game's over at nine." Cass thought a moment. "Anyone caught is tagged or brought back to jail," Cass smiled evilly. He was wearing a comfortable striped short-sleeved shirt, ripped blue jeans and tennis shoes. "If more than half of you get called in before the game ends, we win."

"Ain't nobody going to get called in on our side," Zeke said, dressed in a brightly colored short-sleeved shirt, blue jeans and tennis shoes. Unlike Cass, Zeke was smallish, intelligent looking and slightly handsome.

"Bet it's your parents start calling you in first," Ricky said, joking from beside Cass. He was the big kid and the fighter of the group. Ricky had been suspended half a dozen times last year for one thing or another.

"I think that we have to have a way to prove that we caught them," Eli smiled from behind his BMX bike handlebars.

"What you thinking?" Dewey said with a buck toothed grin.

"I say we take their shoes," Eli said, smiling mischievously.

"That's a good idea," Ricky said.

"So, if we catch you, we are going to take your shoes so you can't say you were never caught," Cass said with a sinister smile.

"We should just strip 'em," said Darryl.

"Calm down," Cass said. "Ain't nobody striping nobody. We take their shoes. Whoever finds Lay though radio me. I want to teach him a lesson."

"We coming for ya," announced Eli, from the seat of his BMX bike.

"Wait," Zeke said. "There's seven of us," Zeke said looking over his team. "You got to give us four to win. You got all the advantages." He looked from his team to Cass and the boys and girls on their bikes. "That's fair."

"We don't believe in fair," Cass said. "But if five of you make it back to old man Johnson's untouched then you win." Cass smiled. He turned to his crew and added, "That means all we got to do is catch three of 'em and we win."

"All right, if we hide until nine o'clock and if we make it back to Johnson's place we win?"

"Right," Cass said.

"All we have to do is have five of us show up at old man Johnson's place by nine and we've beat the Skittles Crew."

Cass sneered. He looked at Lay as if he were something he found on the bottom of his shoe. He pursed his lips and for an instant it looked like he might spit. Instead, he nodded.

"Ain't no one ever beat us, Zeke," Rayshon said, laughing like a jackal.

"We are undefeated," Eli said with a grin, sitting on his bike.

"Who got a watch?"

Greg Porter, who was uninterested in running or riding bikes was wearing a watch. He was the neighborhood kid who lived on the other side of Oak Street and knew everyone, but few knew anything about him.

"I got a watch, and I will tell them when to go," Porter offered. "You need someone to be here at the end? If so, it ain't me. I'm going in at eight thirty. Sorry."

"Think we can figure it out," Cass sneered. Cass grabbed Greg Porter's wrist and looked at the digital watch and nodded. "It's six forty, right now. We'll give you until seven to run and hide. No one can be on old man Johnson's steps before eight forty."

"Get going," said Ricky behind his bike's handlebars.

A little before seven o'clock Zeke and the Starburst Crew took off from in front of the apartment house on the other side of Randolph Street and ran toward Washington Boulevard. They ran to the top of the block, the boundary of the game, and gathered and laid out their grand plan to win the chase.

The runners ran. They split up and some went toward Nineteenth Avenue knowing they had to run through the alleyway which split the houses facing Nineteenth Avenue from the houses facing Twentieth Street. The rules were strictly enforced.

Lay, Zeke and Franky headed toward Twenty-First Street knowing they would have to cut through the alleyway like their counterparts and make their way stealthily toward the far end of Twentieth if possible.

"So, who do you think gets caught first?"

"Darius," Franky said.

"Reg," Lay said with a smile.

Zeke nodded. "I think it will probably be Val," Zeke said craning his neck to see down the alleyway. He paused and so did Franky and Lay.

"You see something?" Franky asked.

"No, I thought I saw something," Zeke said with a shake of his head. "We cool."

"You believe Cass and the others about this being our last summer playing games?"

"I don't know," Lay said unsure.

"It's probably the last summer for them," Zeke said with a smile as the three walked down the alleyway, past garbage cans and the occasional mattress. Behind one house was a broken TV. "They are 'bout to go to the eighth grade and get their driver's license at the same time."

Franky and Lay laughed at Zeke's joke.

"They so stupid that they heard it was chilly outside and all of them grabbed spoons and bowls before going out," Zeke said with a laugh.

Franky and Lay laughed.

"They so stupid when they heard of a quarterback, they thought it was a refund," Zeke said, with a shake of his head.

The three boys made their way down the alleyway. Ahead of them they could hear a dog barking. They slowed and tried to decide if they were going to stay in the alley or cut through a yard.

"Let's cut through this yard," Franky said, looking over the fence and not seeing a dog.

"Yeah, I agree, we can't stay in the alley, you know they are going to come down it eventually."

Zeke agreed and Franky opened the gate and looked left and right and sneaked through the unknown backyard to the gate and fence that led to the Twentieth Street.

"The way I see it, all we have to do is make our way down to the empty parking lot on Saint Charles and wait it out down there before going to Johnson's and winning the Chase."

Franky shushed Zeke and pressed against the side of the house as two BMX bikes raced up the street toward Randolph Avenue. Zeke and Lay looked and caught a glimpse of Eli and Dewey racing by.

"What do we do?" Lay asked, suddenly nervous.

"We run in the opposite direction," Zeke said with a smile. He pushed past Franky and started running down the street with Franky and Lay close behind.

At the corner of Oak Street Zeke turned right and headed toward Nineteenth.

"Where we going?"

"Just follow," Zeke said turning left into the alleyway that ran the length of Twentieth from Oak Street all the way to Randolph.

Once in the alleyway Zeke looked back in the direction they had just run from.

"Think we are okay for now?"

Franky, a little out of breath, wiped his sweating forehead.

"You think they saw us?"

"Naw," Lay said looking back. "If they had, they would have chased us."

"Yeah, we okay for now," Zeke said. "We'll walk up a couple of houses and cut back and forth until we get to that big parking lot at the bottom of Twentieth."

"The old Jewel's parking lot," Franky said.

"What?"

"It used to be a Jewel's grocery store down there," Franky said. "My aunt used to work there."

"Okay," said Zeke with a shake of his head as the trio walked down the alleyway.

"What time is it?"

Franky pulled out his cellphone. He checked the time. "It's just a few minutes 'til eight. We have about an hour to be at old man Johnson's front steps," Franky said.

"Okay, let's get down to the... Jewel's parking lot," Zeke said.

The trio, led by Zeke, snaked their way down the alley in the darkness. The alleyway had dim motion sensor activated lighting from several of the garages that illuminated the area near the garage doors but that was the extent of light in the gravel alley. Once a car turned at the top of the alley and came barreling down the gravel alleyway toward the Randolph Street exit.

Zeke and Franky pressed up against a garage door as the dark car jetted past. On the opposite side of the alley Zeke and Franky saw that Lay had slipped between a fence and garage as the car tore down the narrow alley.

"I say we get out of here," Lay said looking down at the alleyway and the tire tracks that were incredibly close to the tips of his sneakers. "I want to see tomorrow."

The trio cut through a quiet backyard and to the front of the house just a few doors away from Randolph Street. The three cut across the street under the streetlight which cast a wide beam of light and found themselves just one hundred yards from the Jewels parking lot.

The big box store had not been used in years. Lay and Zeke walked to the loading dock and there, on the dock, which looked toward the alleyway they had exited. Just one hundred feet to the right was Twenty-First Street. Before Twenty-First Franky examined the only machinery that remained of the grocery store. The rusted and brown machine looked like an airplane engine, or part of an airplane engine. Above the engine was a metal door that had been welded shut.

"What do you think this is?"

Zeke looked and shook his head.

Lay studied the machine and the welded metal door and thought.

"I think it must be one of those trash compactors," Lay said unsure. "You know you put all the cardboard inside the chute, and it compresses it and ties it up."

Zeke listening smiled.

"It sort of looks like an airplane engine," Franky said.

The trio sat and waited.

"How long you think we got?"

"When do you want to head back to old man Johnson's?"

"I say no sooner than eight thirty," Zeke said.

Franky pulled out his phone and examined it.

"It's only fifteen after eight," Franky said.

"Twenty-five minutes," Lay said to no one in particular.

One minute after Lay's announcement Franky found a broken shopping cart with no wheels and a broken basket. He wanted Zeke and Lay to check it out. They both refused.

The second minute after the time announcement Zeke, bored, got up and walked to the front of the abandoned building. He walked to the other end of the building. He disappeared around the corner under the watchful eyes of Franky and Lay.

"He's dead," Franky said to Lay.

"What?"

"You know that is what happens when someone goes exploring in horror movies?" Franky said with sad confidence.

Lay looked at Franky skeptically.

"You watch too much weird stuff," Lay said with a chuckle.

The third minute Zeke was still gone. Franky and Lay looked at each other and Franky smirked, knowingly.

"Give it a minute," Lay said looking left. "He might be using the bathroom."

Franky looked at Lay and shook his head. "I can't believe you. You know how it goes. Never break up the team. If you need to go to the bathroom you go with a friend. Your friend is supposed to watch your back." He paused. "There's no heroes in a horror movie."

"Again, you need to watch other stuff," Lay said with a shake of his head.

The fifth minute all hell broke loose, well, sort of.

From the far alleyway Zeke, Franky and Lay did not come from came Huey. He, at first was a shadow trying to cross the alleyway that ran from Nineteenth to Twentieth and onto Twenty-First. Under the streetlight Franky and Lay made out Huey's short-sleeve shirt and jeans. He was running toward them like he was being chased.

The two boys tensed for the appearance of boys on bikes behind Huey, but no bikes or boys appeared. Instead, Huey just ran with his arms pumping the air and his legs flailing toward Franky and Lay on the side of the abandoned grocery store.

Before Huey arrived, Zeke reappeared carrying an old and rusty golf club he had found somewhere. Franky and Lay looked at each other and laughed.

"What are you two laughing at?"

"He thought you were dead," Lay said with a laugh.

"I did not think you were dead, I figured you were dead," Franky said. "There is a difference."

Zeke looked at Lay and Franky and was about to say something when Huey arrived nearly in tears.

"What's wrong with you?"

"You worried about your comics?" Asked Franky with a sly smile.

"I got another copy of your comic if we lose," said Lay.

"No, no, that ain't it," Huey said, jittery. He was looking back in the direction he had just run from.

"What's the problem?"

"Man," Huey said, trying to catch his breath and regain his composure. "They ain't playing."

"Who ain't playing?"

"Cass and Ricky," Huey said, looking back frightened.

"What do you mean?" Lay said curious.

"They said they was going for heads. They decided that since this is the last real summer for them, they going to settle some scores."

"What?"

"No," Lay said thinking if Cass had any scores to settle it would be with him.

"Yeah, I was hiding in the alley when they all had a powwow. They were talking about making the game interesting."

"Naw, you heard wrong,"

"Listen, they made plans," Huey said, kneeling. He seemed exhausted. "Cass said Lay was his and his alone. Ricky said he wanted a piece of Lay too, but that Zeke was owed a beatdown. Eli said if he got a chance, he'd definitely wanted to beat the snot out of Darius."

"What about you?"

"Well, Darryl has been looking for a reason to beat the mess out of me for a while," Huey said with a shake of his head. "I got him in trouble in school before the summer, but he ain't going to mess with me as long as Franky is around or Darius." He paused and looked back at Franky. "Right Franky?"

"Yeah, right," Franky said.

"Wait a minute," Zeke said. "I get the settle the score thing but as soon as Ricky steps to me I'm not going to lay down and take it. Ain't nobody just going to take a beating."

"Yeah, they planned on that," Huey said. "They figure if they get two on one or three on one, they can mob us and stomp us out... or worse."

"Damn," Franky said.

"Yeah, damn," Lay said biting at his bottom lip.

"So, what do you think we should do?"

Zeke looked back at Huey and Franky. Lay had climbed off the loading dock and was already walking down the alleyway.

"Hey, we going this way," Zeke said pointing with his golf club.

Lay looked back and reversed course. Zeke, Huey and Franky walked toward Oak Street. Lay followed.

"You got a plan?"

Zeke looked at Lay and there, behind his eyes, there was doubt. Lay nodded. He fell quiet. He looked back and watched the street they had been on diminish as they headed toward Twentieth First.

Chapter 17. 8:40

The four friends ran down Oak toward the next township only to stop at Twenty First and race up the unfamiliar street. They took in the single-family homes and the manicured yards, bushes separated homes and yards from each other. The thick bushes rose to three or four feet, but few were taller. In the front yards were the squares of green and walkways from the sidewalk to the front porches and back to the unseen backyards.

"We can't stay on this street too long," Zeke, the oldest of the four said still holding onto the rusted golf club. He was taller than either Huey, Lay or Franky. Dressed in short-sleeved T-shirt, jeans and sneakers, he ran confidently down the sidewalk toward the end of the block with long and loping strides. Behind him ran the scared Huey, Lay and Franky. Huey and Franky were a little thicker in body than Lay.

Huey was dark and the color of milk chocolate and dressed in short-sleeved T-shirt and jeans. On his feet were tennis shoes.

Franky was a lighter shade of sandalwood with a medium box cut and thick eyebrows. He had a single dimple on his left cheek. He was dressed in a brightly colored striped short-sleeve T-shirt and jeans.

At the corner, Zeke slowed and stretched out his arms and the golf club to slow Huey, Lay and Franky. He peeked right looking for any of the boys on their bikes. He took a step forward and waved them ahead as he ran across the street to the next corner.

On the corner Zeke ran up to the third house and turned up the walkway and climbed the steps to the elevated stone porch. The house was distinct in its architecture. It was setback from the sidewalk and red brick. The house looked to be two stories. On the ground floor was a doorway. Yet, Zeke, Huey, Franky and Lay had bypassed the ground floor door and climbed to the second-floor porch which hid them.

"Who lives here?" Asked Lay, curious.

"No one, right now," said Zeke, looking around. "I think the owner died."

"What?"

"How you know?" Asked Franky, uncertain.

"My mom and dad were looking at it, when it came on the market," Zeke said. "It is bigger than our house."

"Yeah, it is bigger than most houses on our street."

"Think the owner's ghost is roaming around inside?"

"Don't be stupid," Zeke said with a laugh. "There ain't no such thing as ghosts."

"There is too," Franky said.

Lay did not weigh in. He watched as Zeke, Huey and Franky stared at each other silently. The quiet grew. Lay let his head rest on his fist as he leaned against the porch wall.

"You know there are ghosts," Huey said. "I know our ancestors are all around us."

"What?"

"I mean it," Huey said. "They watch over us. I mean, they watch over the kids. I think they gave up on the adults." Huey paused. "I think we still hear them."

Lay chuckled at the idea.

"What you laughing at?"

"I wish there was somebody watching over us," Lay said with a jaded expression. "With all this stuff going on and you telling us that Cass and Ricky got plans for us, we need a little help."

Franky and Huey nodded.

"Remember when things were easier?" Zeke asked.

"Remember? We're only eleven. When were things easier? When we were babies?" Huey chuckled.

"No, I mean, before things started to get serious," Zeke said to Huey.

"When was that?" Huey said with a tilt of his head.

"Things have always been serious," Franky said. "I mean, here, on Twentieth, with my friends' things aren't as serious, but they still are... serious. Sometimes."

"Yeah, sometimes," Franky said.

Lay nodded, looking up. He had a thought but didn't want to say anything.

"I mean, remember when all we did was play and have fun?"

"You mean when we were six or seven?"

"No, I mean when we could just play and not worry about stupid stuff," Zeke said, frustrated for some reason.

No one responded.

"You know we are breaking the rules hiding out over here?" Franky said.

"Shut up," Huey said. "You mean you ain't never broke a rule?"

Franky closed his mouth. Zeke smiled, knowing the truth. Huey nodded.

"We ain't staying here," Zeke said to Franky. "We just taking a minute. We about to get back in the game."

"See, Franky, you was just talking about taking things too serious," Huey said.

"Yeah, huh," said Zeke.

"Jay told me that because of who we are we are seen as adults quicker than anyone else," Lay said timidly. "So, everyone around us is always trying to prepare us to be seen as adults even if we aren't."

"What's that mean?"

"I think it means that they are making us grow up faster than we should," Lay said sadly.

"Yeah, I don't want to grow up too fast," Huey said.

"Me either," said Franky.

"I don't know if we get to choose," Zeke said.

"Yeah, there are too many people trying to make us grow up faster than we want," Lay said with little emotion. "I mean, we are playing a game where we are running for our lives." He shook his head. He took a breath and added. "We are so screwed up."

"It's sort of fun," Franky said.

"It would be more fun if someone wasn't trying to go all Candyman on us."

Everyone nodded at Huey's words.

"Well, what do we do?"

No one answered. Zeke looked to Lay. Franky looked to Zeke and then to Huey. Huey looked to Franky and then to Lay. Lay looked up and found everyone looking to him.

"Why you looking at me?"

"You got the number one psycho gunning for you," Zeke said with a serious tone. "I know Franky. I know Huey. I figure of us all you might have a plan."

Huey and Franky looked at each other and then at Zeke. Huey frowned at Zeke and punched him in the shoulder. Franky shook his head. Huey and Franky leaned close to Lay.

Lay bit his lip, thinking.

"What time is it?"

Franky fished out his phone.

With thirty minutes until they had to be at Johnson's house, they found a place to lay low. They were hiding in one of the handful of garages in the alley between Twentieth and Twenty-First Street just one hundred feet from Oak Street. It was one of the rickety garages that needed to be torn down and rebuilt. The garage door was closed but there was a corner of the door which sat awkwardly against the frame. That two-foot-wide opening was how the four boys entered the rickety two car garage. There were no cars in the dark, quiet and cool interior of the garage.

"I don't know about this place," Lay said once inside.

"Relax," said Franky. He was sitting on a pair of stacked bald truck tires.

"This place may fall on our heads," Lay said studying the ramshackle garage and its rotting timbers. "It looks like a deathtrap."

"I thought you were some kind of badass," Huey said. He had found a box and was sitting on it.

"This ain't our new clubhouse," Zeke said minus his golf club. He was scanning the interior of the garage for something. He paused. "We're here, just for now."

"We'll move out in a few minutes. Trying to give the hunters a chance to give up and start to head to Twentieth," Lay said offering a choice.

He looked around the shell of a garage and walked to one of the windows.

"So, tell me again who's on who's hit list," Zeke said to Huey.

"Well, like I said you got Ricky looking for you. Cass and Ricky are looking to stomp Lay out. Cass told everyone he wants Lay," Huey said. He paused, thinking. "Darryl said that he wanted to put a hurting on me," Huey said with a head shake. "Rayshon said he wanted to stomp the snot out of Franky." Huey said as he looked at Franky in the darkness sitting on the tire. "Hey Franky, what did you do to make Rayshon want to stomp you out?"

Franky shrugged his shoulders in answer.

"Come on, give," Zeke said.

"Well, he was copying off this kid in class and I told the teacher and he got in trouble," Franky said.

"Let me guess," Zeke said, with a growing smile. "You were the kid Rayshon was copying off?"

Franky crossed his arms in front of him and leaned back against the wall of the garage and tried to get comfortable.

Zeke, Lay and Huey looked at Franky.

"I didn't do the homework for him to copy," Franky said as an answer.

Lay smiled and chuckled at Franky's honesty. He walked to the rear of the garage and the only door in the garage and tried it. The door gave and opened a crack. Lay looked out and into the dark and quiet backyard.

"Any dogs out there?"

Lay looked back and shook his head at Huey.

"If there were dogs out there, they would have been barking already," Lay said with a slight grin. He left the door open a crack, for a quick getaway, just in case.

"You know, when the cold weather comes, and it's coming, this garage going to fall," said Franky.

"I think it'll be fine in the cold," Zeke said, looking at the rotting wood. He tried to peel off a piece. The wood was rotting but not rotten. "If it goes its going under the weight of the first snow."

"Man, we in the last days of summer and trying to shut up Cass and his bad boys and you fools are talking about winter already," Huey said.

"Winter is coming," said Zeke ominously.

Franky looked at Zeke confused. Huey shook his head. Lay prepared for the last twenty minutes of the Chase.

Chapter 18. 8:45

"The way I see it is they can't get us all if we split up," Lay explained.

"Yeah, we all split up and make our way to old man Johnson's' house." Franky said with a nod of his head.

"I don't know," said Huey, unsure.

"It makes the most sense," Lay said calmly. "Besides, according to Huey if you and me split up that means Cass and Ricky can't get both of us."

"Yeah, all I have to worry about is Darryl," Huey said, with a timid smile.

"The only one I have to look out for is stupid Rayshon," Franky said. He added, "You two have the targets on your backs, but I would not want to be you Lay if either Ricky or Cass catch up with you."

"Yeah," Huey agreed.

"You know Cass is cra-zay. He's likely to do anything."

"I think he caught up with Mar Mar after the fight and now Mar Mar is missing," Franky said.

"I don't believe that," Zeke said. "Them Nineteenth Avenue boys ain't soft. I can't see Mar Mar getting got by Cass no matter how crazy he is."

"Yeah," Huey said. "Cass ain't no ninja assassin."

"I'm saying."

"So, there's four of us and four ways to get to old man Johnson's," Lay said logically. There was the alleyway they were in on the westside of Underwood. There was the most direct route straight down Twentieth Street. One could be on the left side and one on the right side. The last route was the alleyway closest to Nineteenth Avenue.

"I would either go down the alleyway and then cut across a backyard and hope to be near Randolph Street before the bikes see you or down the far alleyway," Lay said as an explanation. He paused and added, "Maybe the most unexpected way might be the safest. Can't imagine they would expect anyone to just walk down Twentieth all big and bad and bold." Lay shook the thought from his head.

With fifteen minutes left in the game Zeke, Huey and Franky exited the garage. Franky was the first to leave.

"See you at old man Johnson's," Franky said and vanished from the garage through the small exit.

The second was Zeke.

"Don't do anything I wouldn't do," Zeke said and followed Franky. He folded his taller body and was swallowed up in the darkness.

After Zeke left then Huey squeezed out of the two-foot space.

"See you on the other side," Huey said and smiled to Lay. He slipped out of the garage leaving Lay in the dilapidated garage. He kept looking at the door he had left open, just in case and thought of going through the unknown backyard and onto Twentieth Street just a few houses from the corner of Randolph Street.

Left in the garage Lay understood why he was last. Lay thought about what Zeke had said. Ricky and Cass were both looking for him. If he avoided those two then he was guaranteed to get to old man Johnson's house unmolested. As he stood in the quiet garage Lay tried to think what his next steps were to get to old man Johnson house.

All he had to do was step out of the garage, just to the northside of Oak Street and three houses to the house on the corner of Twentieth Street. Once at that house Lay would be at the top of Oak Street and Twentieth Street. At the top of Twentieth Street, he would have to make a decision on the three routes possible.

Twentieth was divided equally in half by the Beck's house in Lay's mind. There were five houses, including the weird Victorian hotel on the side of the Beck's house, on the westside and at the north end of the street. Below the Beck's house were five more houses that included the Stewart sisters house and the last house on the block.

On the eastside of Twentieth Street near Oak Street sat Cass's house. Across the street from the Beck's was Val's house. Two houses down from Val's house was old man Johnson's house.

Lay took a full minute to decide he was going to go out the garage door and through the backyard of the unknown house. He pushed the door open a little more to exit and padded across the dark backyard where he could see the outlines of lawn furniture. He moved as quietly as possible, despite there being no lights on in the house as he reached the wooden gate. Lay opened the gate slowly and as quietly as possible and once he opened the gate he stepped out of the backyard and closed the gate hoping for no noise.

He fast walked along the side of the house and in a minute, he was on the sidewalk of Twentieth looking left and right for any activity.

The street was quiet and Lay stayed in the shadows and pools of darkness afforded by the half dozen streetlights on each street.

Walking everso stealthily toward Oak Street Lay expected to hear bicycles bearing down on him any second. No bicycle riders rode up from Randolph. No bicycle riders were visible on Twentieth. Lay hesitated. It could not be this easy.

•••

Val came bounding from the Beck's backyard and was almost mowed down by Ricky as she ran into the front yard. She simply dove to the left as Ricky raced up the small rise of grass and crashed into the bushes. Stuck momentarily, Val battle rolled and nimbly climbed to her feet and looked left and right, like she was crossing the street, and ran untouched across the street to the safety of Mister Johnson's steps. Reg stood on the steps and smiled like he had won the lottery as Val sat a few steps below him, tired.

"Damn girl," Ricky said with a growl.

"What's his problem?"

"I could not tell you all of them," Val said with a smile.

Reg smiled and nodded in response.

Ricky rode up the street toward Saint Charles.

"Where are the others?"

"On their way, I guess," Reg said unsure.

Franky came loping around the corner followed by an out of breath Rayshon. Franky looked back and smiled at the pathetic effort by Rayshon to catch him. He slowed and started to walk down the street like he was out for a Saturday night stroll. Franky had this cockiness about him. He was not overly big but not the smallest in the Starburst Crew. He might have been any kid from the block but play a game against him and Franky transformed. He was incredibly competitive and probably the best athlete in the Starburst Crew.

Franky sat on the steps of Mister Johnson's house and was the third member to arrive.

"All we need is two more and we've won," said Reg with a smile.

Zeke appeared near the McKay's house and ran as fast as he could toward Mister Johnson's house. Behind him raced Ricky and Eli. Ricky reached out and nearly caught Zeke. Eli pulled up as Zeke reached Mister Johnson's house and stepped onto the steps.

"Good job," Franky said.

Val climbed to the top of the steps and sat with her back to the screen door.

"Where is Huey and Lay?" Reg asked, looking around for the others.

"Yeah," said Val curious.

"They got Huey in the alley behind Mister Watson's house. They beat him up pretty bad," Zeke said with a shake of his head. "It was not cool. We tried to stop 'em, but they were on some other level stuff for some reason. I don't know what really happened."

"Who got Huey?" Reg asked.

"What do you mean, you don't know what happened?" Val asked, narrowing her eyes at Zeke.

"I can't say," Franky said. "I was running for old man Johnson's house and when I turned saw Rayshon trying to catch me," Franky said. "I just ran as fast as I could."

Val looked at Zeke.

Zeke looked away guilty.

"You ran?"

"I didn't have a choice," Zeke said.

"We always have a choice," Val said with venom in her voice.

"We were supposed to split up and we ended up running down the same alley. It was a stupid move. When we crossed Oak Street, I heard their bikes and began running. It all just happened so fast."

"You just left him?"

"What choice did I have? To get caught and beat up too? Huey was running and when he figured he was caught he tried to play like he was a ninja and hide in the shadows or something. We told him that wasn't going to work, but he said he had a plan." Zeke paused, frustrated. "That plan didn't work."

"What happened?"

"I told you, we were in the alley, just over there." Zeke pointed toward Twenty-First. "We had run toward the park at first and then made our way back to Twentieth. We," Zeke said, pausing to catch his breath.

"Who *we?*"

"Well, it was me, Huey and Franky and that's it," Zeke said.

Val didn't speak for a long time.

"Rayshon showed up at the end of the alley," Zeke said. "They boxed us in."

"How come you didn't jump a fence?"

"Franky was further down the alley and gone and I just avoided Rayshon. I think Huey was the furthest back when Rayshon showed up," Zeke said.

"I said that," Franky said.

"Why didn't you go back?"

"What?"

"You know go back and help," Val said, angry.

"Things just happened so fast," Zeke said, stammering. "We weren't like... next to each other. We were... separated. So, Rayshon came barreling down on me and I dodged him." Zeke smiled at the memory. "I dodged Rayshon. When I dodged him, I ran to the gate where Franky had gone and decided to go down to Randolph."

"Wait," Val said suddenly. She was sitting on the top step of Mister Johnson's front steps. Behind her was the aluminum screen door which barred the entrance to the Victorian where Mister Johnson lived. "Okay, you and Huey got trapped."

"Yep," Zeke said.

"Why didn't you stay and help?"

"I didn't tell you that behind us Darryl and Ricky showed up all Mad Max and the Thunderdome?" Zeke said.

At the sound of Ricky's name Val's lip jerked like she had a fishhook in it. Val thinned her big brown eyes and stared at Zeke before speaking.

"So, what happened?"

"Like I said, Rayshon races past me and I turn and watch as Rayshon boxes Huey in. I thought they were going to grab his shoes, but it wasn't like that."

"What do you mean?"

"Darryl climbed off his bike and he and Ricky beat up Huey like nobody's business."

Val thought and did not speak.

"Somebody needs to go and check on Huey," Val said, finally.

Zeke looked down at the tops of his shoes. Franky did not move for fear of someone thinking him volunteering to go check on Huey.

"He could be really hurt," Val said.

"All right, I'll go, but if I get beat down, I want you to know you all suck not going with me," Zeke said disgusted. He climbed down the stairs and looked left and right into the darkness. Huey was at the far end of Twentieth in the alley on the westside of the block. The quickest way to the alley was straight across from old man Johnson's house and through Missus Allen's backyard.

Zeke ran as fast as he could across the street and into Missus Allen's backyard and disappeared in the darkness.

Tamra Mills was all of eleven years old and brown as a peanut and smart. She was the youngest child of three and curious. All her girlfriends had laughed at Tamra when they found out she had not kissed a boy.

"What are you waiting for?"

"It ain't that bad," said Felicia, her closest friend. "You might as well get it over with and prepare for seventh grade."

Those words rang in her head as she rode around on her bike playing a stupid end of the summer game with neighborhood kids. Tamra had overheard the big plans Cass and Ricky were hatching and didn't care. She had no beef with any of the boys they were playing against. If she had any funk, it was with Ricky and Eli. They were always slapping her on her butt when they got a chance.

Tamra thought about that too as she rode her bike down Twentieth toward Saint Charles Avenue looking for Darius.

She found Zeke heading toward Nineteenth and caught up with him at the alley's mouth that split the east side of Nineteenth Avenue.

"Zeke, you seen Darius?"

"Why?"

"I'm looking for him," Tamra said with an easy smile, sitting on her mountain bike.

"I haven't," Zeke said and walked down the alleyway.

Tamra shook her head at Zeke and rode back toward Twenty-First and the alleyway on that side which separated the eastside of Twentieth from the westside of Twenty-First.

She had seen Reg and asked him the same question.

"Last time I saw him he was up near Randolph," Reg said. He cut through a backyard and disappeared.

Tamra rode up to Randolph and ran into Dewey, who was sitting in front of a house a few houses from the corner.

"Dewey, you seen Darius?"

"I'm looking for Reg the Egg," Dewey said, with a smirk.

"I saw him down near Saint Charles," Tamra said. "He was in the alley coming up the side closest to two one."

"Okay," Dewey said and started to pedal off.

"Hey, have you seen Darius?"

Dewey rode away. Tamra pouted.

"Try on Randolph near the Baker house," Dewey shouted. He had stopped in the middle of the street. Tamra nodded as Dewey rode down the street.

Tamra pedaled toward the Baker's house. It was a distinct house in the Underwood. It was one of those houses which should have been in a magazine. There was a gate around it. In the front was a circular driveway. Tamra pedaled to the alleyway entrance and knew Darius would not be on Twenty-First Street. Being on Twenty-First Street was against the rules.

She looked down the alleyway and, in the darkness, just made out someone ducking into a backyard. Tamra pedaled back to Twentieth and turned her mountain bike down the quiet street looking for the boy that had tried to escape her.

The boy appeared on the sidewalk just twenty feet away from Tamra. Tamra pedaled as fast as she could and was shoulder to shoulder with the running boy. He turned his head to see Tamra and Tamra turned her mountain bike and the front wheel hit the curb, bounced over it and sent the girl flying toward the startled boy.

The pair collided and fell in a twist of legs and arms in the front lawn of someone's house.

"Damn, girl, you nearly killed me," Darius Hutchinson said, pushing Tamra off him. He was unwrapping Tamra's legs from his when Tamra sat up and looked at Darius in the dark.

Darius Hutchinson had a tight fade crowning his oval shaped face. He had ears that stuck out and were level with his big brown eyes. He also had a straight nose and full lips that always seemed to be in a permanent smirk. He was eleven and skinny. Dressed in his cartoon T-shirt, cutoff jeans and sneakers he seemed about to laugh.

Before Tamra could talk herself out of it, she leaned in and kissed Darius Hutchinson on the lips. She kissed him and waited for horns to blow or bells to ring. The kiss was just a kiss. Nothing else.

Tamra Mills pulled back and there was Darius Hutchinson sitting on the lawn unmoved and shocked.

Tamra climbed to her feet and grabbed her mountain bike and rode away.

Chapter 19. 8:50

The alleyway on the eastside of Twentieth was deserted when Zeke made his way through the quiet backyard of Missus Allen. The wooden gate enclosed the manicured backyard and the two trees that sat in the rear of the house. Zeke looked to the right and saw that Missus Allen had a gazebo-like tent where the outlines of chairs sat. She must entertain her friends there, Zeke thought as he moved as quietly as possible through the quiet backyard. A third of the backyard was devoted to the two walls of the garage Zeke saw. The leader of the Starburst crew edged along the walkway past the garage and to the rear gate of the property.

On the other side of the gate Zeke found himself under the light of one of the alley streetlights. The streetlight cast a wide beam that fell on the front of Missus Allen's garage door her neighbors across the alley. The light faded maybe ten feet in either direction concentrating its beam on garages. Zeke stepped into the alleyway and noted the garbage cans. Most of the cans were made of that heavy duty dark green plastic with the matching lids. Yet, as Zeke walked toward Oak, he did see a few of the older, beaten up metallic cans.

Why were people buying those metal cans now? Zeke thought. They were not better than the plastic ones. They didn't last as long. When the snow got the metal cans they froze. When the snow melted the cans rusted. Zeke thought all this as he walked up the alleyway being a bit of a can expert. His mother had made him start taking out the garbage when he was seven and it had been his job ever since.

Zeke thought about how he persuaded his mother to make his father switch the three metal garbage cans he had bought when they first moved into the house. His father, a tough man, would not have listened to Zeke. So, Zeke had to convince his mother of the value of the plastic garbage can. A week or two after Zeke had talked to his mother his father came home with new dark green plastic garbage cans.

Zeke thought all this as he walked up the alley looking for Huey.

A noise from the dark made Zeke stop. It was late and dark. Anything could be in the alley. He had seen rats running in the alley in the early morning when he went to take out the garbage. His dad had told him that he had seen a rat as big as a cat fighting a dog in Detroit a long time ago, but Zeke just thought his dad was trying to scare him.

The noise, more like a howl, stopped Zeke again. He wanted to turn around and go back to old man Johnson's house, but he took a deep breath and moved to the far side of the alley and hurried forward.

As he tried not to look at what was making the noise, he noticed a foot and leg in the darkness. It was Huey. Zeke stopped his fast walk and cut across the alley to his friend. He was beaten badly. Huey was propped up against a chain-link fence. He had taken a beating.

"Hey, Huey, I'm going to get you back home," Zeke said.

He lifted Huey to his feet and Zeke noted Huey was all cut up and bleeding.

"All right, you think you can hold on if I put you on my back?"

Huey nodded.

"Okay, if you can't I can fireman carry you," Zeke said.

"My side hurts," Huey said painfully.

"Yeah, they stomped you out," Zeke said.

He leaned down and Huey gingerly climbed on Zeke's back.

"Don't choke me," Zeke said. "Here we go," he said as he walked, carrying Huey on his back to the end of the fence and through the yard they were behind.

Luckily, Huey's house was only a few houses from where Zeke had found him.

•••

With nine o'clock just a few minutes away the Skittles Crew prowled the front of old man Johnson's house like shark waiting for blood. In the alleyway behind old man Johnson's were Rayshon and Darryl.

"Where are they?"

No one answered.

"All we have to do is wait," Eli said.

"I'm okay with that," Dewey said.

"You would be okay with that," Ricky said.

"What's that suppose to mean?"

"Dewey, go and tell Darryl to come up here. You stay with Rayshon," Cass said with a growl.

Dewey pedaled his bike to the rear of Johnson's place.

Darryl rode around the house walkway and to the front.

Val, Reg and Franky noted Darryl race by from the back of old man Johnson's house. He met up with Cass and Ricky.

"We just wait," Cass said. "Spread out. They got to come to us."

Cass was parked on the sidewalk one house up from old man Johnson's house. Eli was on the opposite sidewalk, closest to the Beck's house, looking around for any movement. Behind them were Ricky and Darryl. Around Darryl's bike handlebars were Huey's sneakers. Ricky was sitting on his BMX bike looking for anyone to come from Randolph. Darryl was just on the other side of the sidewalk, near the Stewart sister's house.

"They waiting for Darius and Lay," Val said, seeing the situation they were watching on the street.

"What time is it?"

"Time for you to get a watch," Reg said.

"It's eight fifty-three," Darius said. Darius appeared from behind Mister Johnson's house, Tamra following close behind on her mountain bike.

"What the what," said Reg as he looked from the street to the side of the house. Tamra leaned her bike against the bushes and sat on the steps with Darius. Darius grinned.

"Figures," Val said and shook her head. She smiled and crossed her arms in front of her chest with a deep breath.

Reg laughed. "That's why you didn't go after me, earlier?"

"Did we win?" Asked Darius.

"Did we win?" Asked Tamra, with a smile.

"Not even close," Val said. "There's only three of us here, four with you Darius," she continued. "Zeke is in the wind. Huey is MIA. No one 's seen Lay. Our chances are slim, you ask me," Val said with a smirk.

A whistle broke the conversation up.

Ricky and Eli raced their bikes past old man Johnson's house to where Cass and Darryl were posted. Val climbed to her feet and looked in the direction of all the activity. Reg stood and then Franky.

"What is it?"

"It's Lay," Val said. She was the first to see Lay. He was walking down the middle of Twentieth just as casual and matter of fact. He might have been leading a parade and not seemed so important or special.

"Really?"

"Yeah, he's just walking down the street as cool as a cucumber," Val said from her vantage point.

Chapter 20. 8:55

Cass was named after Cassius Clay. His father loved Cassius Clay. He knew Cassius Clay had denounced his slave name and become Muhammad Ali later in life but it did not sway his father from naming his son after one of the greatest boxers in the world. When Cass was old enough to learn where he got his name his father was gone. It was just his mother, his older brother Kenard and him. His mother worked for a realtor and was never around. She was trying to chase her dreams. His brother, never too industrious, got in trouble in and out of school. He had gone to jail a couple of times and been given probation. His brother nearly twenty had decided to beat the man. He had all these dreams and plans, and nothing seemed to pan out. It was always because of the man. So, as Cass grew older and more bitter, raised mostly by himself and his friends, he became uninterested in school. He was twelve and going on eighteen, in his mind and ready to be a man. It didn't matter that he was ill-prepared to be an adult. He just wanted to be out the house making money and running things. None of that mattered as Cass smiled and handed his bike to Eli and walked toward Lay. He had learned to solve all his problems himself with his fists and if his fists weren't enough, he would rely on something else.

"You know I been looking forward to this all night," Cass said with an evil smile. He was dressed in his short-sleeve T-shirt, jeans and sneakers. Around his neck was a thin gold chain.

Lay did not speak. The words he thought to say would fall on deaf ears. So, he walked and figured this would squash all the bad blood between him and Cass or at least decide who was a punk and who wasn't.

Ricky and Darryl pulled their bikes onto the sidewalk to enjoy the show. Rayshon and Eli, with Cass's bike pulled to the other side of the street to watch the fireworks. Everyone at old man Johnson's house were drawn to the action.

Cass walked up casually toward Lay with that smug smile on his face and as he got within arm's reach he ran forward. Lay wasn't expecting that. Cass's face was all Lay could see.

He was punched on the side of the head and then hit on the chin. Cass was all fire. Lay felt a punch hit him in the chest and without memory or any sensation other than stinging pain he was backpedaling. Cass kept swinging heavy blows. He was trying to knock Lay's head off his shoulders. The cost of those heavy blows was Cass slowed just long enough in the attack for Lay to go bouncing off the fender of a parked car and out of Cass's reach for a moment.

"Where did your punk ass go?"

Cass looked back at his crew and turned back and kept coming. He stepped between the two parked cars he had punched Lay through, cautiously. He was looking for the boy who threatened his Twentieth Street credibility.

On the side of the parked car Cass found Lay. The smaller boy had a hand on the car for stability. Cass flew at Lay all fists and elbows.

Lay blinked and realized he had bounced off the trunk of a car and onto the hood of another. Cass had paused at the sight of Lay ping ponging from one car to the other.

Cass turned and smiled.

"Look at this fool," Cass said with a cackle. "I think he was just lucky with you Ricky," Cass laughed.

"Yeah, he was lucky," Ricky said with a laugh.

That short brag gave Lay just enough time to recover. He rested his hand on the car hood and narrowed his focus. He backed up and nearly tripped over the lip of the curb. He was disoriented. Lay had come south from the top of Oak Street before the fight began and now, he was going backward.

He put his hand on the side of the car for stability and backed up. His feet felt a little heavy suddenly. He could not afford to trip and fall. In the back of his mind Lay knew if he went down Cass was going to stomp him out. So, Lay refused to go down.

"Where you going, pretender?"

Cass stepped onto the sidewalk and Lay finding the end of the car stepped off the curb and back into the street.

"He scared, Cass," Eli said with a laugh.

"He don't want no more of you," Rayshon said.

Lay shook his head and took a deep breath to clear the cobwebs from his brain. He waited for Cass to follow him into the street. Cass, all confident and fearless stepped into the street and rushed Lay again.

Lay was ready. At least, he was prepared for Cass's attack.

Cass threw a short left to get Lay's attention, but it was the overhand right that was coming to knock his head off. Lay sidestepped the launched bomb.

Cass left himself open and Lay threw a flurry of punches into Cass's side.

Cass immediately winced like he had been stabbed. Cass spun with his elbow pressed against his side where Lay had hit him. Cass stared at Lay with death in his eyes.

"You think you doing something?"

Lay did not talk. He had nothing to say. He wanted to rush forward and end this, but his uncle had taught him to be patient. Cass was still dangerous.

Cass took a deep breath and peeled his elbow, painfully from his side.

"Bring the heat," someone said behind Lay.

"Don't let that punk punk you," another voice said.

Lay did not look back. Whoever was talking wasn't fighting. They were spectating.

Lay circled Cass. Cass snarled.

"I'm going to teach you, pretender," Cass said stepping forward and put on a surprising burst of speed to close on Lay. He lowered his head and Lay swung a punch at the charging forehead. Cass lifted his head, crashing that rock hard head into Lay's mouth. Lay pushed away from Cass and into the arms of Rayshon.

"Get off me," the Twentieth Street kid said, pushing him back toward Cass.

Lay was thrown toward Cass.

Cass was smiling in the middle of the street as Lay came toward him with a cut lip. Cass reached out and as he did Lay used a technique his uncle had taught him and swam through the outstretched arms and bear hugged Cass.

Surprised by Lay's attack Cass tried to free himself from Lay's grip. Lay held onto Cass just long enough to orient himself to his surroundings. He shoved Cass away near the middle of the block.

Even though it was night the commotion on the street drew the attention of many that lived on Twentieth Street.

Lay pulled in a deep breath and prepared for Cass's next attack. This time he was prepared for the little burst of speed Cass used to throw off Lay.

Cass smiled an evil smile.

"You want this to be one of those viral fights?" Cass smiled to the cameras filming. "I'm good with that."

Cass's right arm seemed to be looser than before when Lay had hit him in the side. Cass stretched his arms to their full length and as before he jumped and put on a display of speed that brought him close to Lay. Cass swung a left hook toward Lay's head that the eleven-year-old ducked.

Lay ducked the punch and fired three or four shots into Cass's midsection. He backed away from the powerful right that grazed the top of his head.

Lay expected Cass to continue his attack but when he looked up Cass was standing there wheezing and trying to catch his breath.

Kill the stomach to kill the head.

Lay circled Cass, looking for the finishing shot.

Before Lay could finish the fight Ricky stepped forward. He had been patiently waiting for a rematch.

"Thought this was between me and Cass," Lay said seeing Ricky moving toward him.

"Naw," Ricky said. "You sucker punched me. I promised when the time was good, I would get my revenge."

Lay smiled and nodded. He looked at Cass and watched as the Twentieth Street tough seemed stuck like a fly on flypaper in the spot. He seemed to be having a hard time breathing.

"Cass, I didn't want this fight with you," Lay said watching Ricky approach. "I just wanted to finish it."

Ricky ran forward and tried to tackle Lay. Lay stepped in front of Cass as Ricky adjusted his run and ran toward him. When Ricky picked up speed and was nearly on top of Lay, Lay deftly stepped out of the way and allowed Ricky to bowl over Cass. Cass and Ricky went crashing into the front fender and wheel of the parked car behind them.

Lay shook his head.

Ricky jumped up and spun around. Lay turned to the approaching Ricky. Ricky ran and slowed down as he got close to Lay.

Lay threw out a soft right-hand punch and Ricky stepped left. Lay threw another predictable left and Ricky moved right. Lay circled Ricky waiting for Ricky's attack.

Ricky stepped forward and threw a right-handed hook that if it had connected would have torn Lay's head off. Unfortunately for Ricky,

Lay stepped out of the arc of the hook and behind it and fired a left-right-left combination to Ricky's unguarded midsection.

As before, Ricky dropped to his knees.

"No sucker punch," Lay said under his breath. "You're just bad at this."

Lay looked at the two crumpled Skittles and shook his head.

Darryl stepped forward.

Lay narrowed his dark eyes.

"You sure you want this?"

Darryl stopped in his tracks. Behind him Eli and Rayshon climbed on their bikes and rode away. Darryl looked back and seeing his friends gone hesitated.

Cass managed to stand up, a little worse from wear. Ricky was climbing to his feet as well.

Remember you can't let a bully think you're soft, or they will keep coming at you forever, his uncle had told him.

Lay walked to Ricky and stopped. Ricky reached up a hand Lay brushed away like an annoying gnat in his face.

"You deserve worse than this, but I got other things to worry about," Lay said and punched Ricky hard enough to put the bigger boy down by the parked car.

Lay looked back at Darryl who was still in the exact spot he was before. He turned and found Cass on his feet and in his hand, his pocketknife.

"Come on, pretender," Cass said more spite than voice. He had the knife in his right hand and holding it like a magic wand.

Lay seeing the knife tried to remember what his uncle had taught him about weapons. They had trained for any situation. Of course, the hardest lesson was weapons.

Pay attention. This lesson could save your life. If someone has a weapon they are going to try and hurt or kill you. That is a fact. You have to decide are you willing to be hurt and live or allow them to kill you. If you aren't afraid of getting hurt, then you will probably survive. No one is Superman. No one is faster than a speeding bullet.

Lay's uncle's words rang in his head as he squared off with Cass and the pocketknife.

Cass wasn't as spry as before, but he was dangerous because of the pocketknife. Lay knew that if Cass tried to rush him, he had to disarm him or die.

If you aren't afraid of getting hurt, then you will probably survive.

Cass snarled and took a few quick steps toward Lay with his knife hand slashing as he moved. Lay did not take his eyes off the pocketknife. A little slower than before Cass jumped toward Lay and Lay allowed him. He concentrated on the right arm and hand of Cass. Cass punched Lay but Lay did not care about his left hand or the punch. Lay instead blocked the left hand and then grabbed for Cass's right. As soon as he gripped Cass's right hand Lay twisted it backwards and watched the pocketknife go spinning into the dark.

Lay turned and found himself hip-to-hip with Cass. He kicked backwards and swept Cass's legs from under him. Cass fell heavily on the street. Lay stepped over Cass and paused just long enough to make sure

Darryl had not moved and Ricky was still near the parked car. They were exactly where Lay had last seen them.

"This is over," Lay said and instead of stomping Cass the eleven-year-old walked away from the three boys and toward the Starburst crew who were watching.

Chapter 21. Aftermath

Old man Johnson's house was the base and the last place to go for the Starburst crew to meet up and gather after the end of the Chase. The old Victorian sat silently and quietly observed the events on Twentieth. Old man Johnson's house sat on two lots of land that created an incredible expanse of green grass between the house and the next house three houses from Randolph Street. The Victorian had been the home to a celebrity long ago, or so the stories went. Now, it was owned by William Johnson, a doctor who liked throwing parties during the summer and going to Florida during the winter. Yet, the Starburst crew knew very little about old man Johnson other than he was rarely home during the weekends, their prime playtime.

Just before nine the Starburst crew celebrated the defeat of Cass and Ricky with Lay. In the background Eli, Darryl, Dewey and Rayshon grabbed their defeated leader and bruised and beaten friends. Rayshon and Eli took Cass. Dewey and Darryl took the still bent over Ricky and slinked into the dark.

The Starburst crew mobbed Lay as the Skittles crew walked and pedaled their bikes away from their latest defeat. Val was the first to arrive at Lay's side.

Val hugged Lay. Lay winced as the girl with the short curls that fell over her forehead and almond shaped eyes hugged him. She had big cheeks and full lips and held onto Lay like he was a door handle. Lay tried to smile at Val. He tried to smile finding Val so close. But for all of her enthusiasm her hugs were painful as she seemed to find all the spots Cass had hit and injured.

"I'm so proud of you," Val said, with a big toothy grin.

Lay nodded and pushed Val back gently.

Franky had somehow gotten Huey's sneakers from Darryl's bike and had them over his shoulder. He hugged and hooked his arm around Lay's neck. Lay winced with Franky's hug. Val delicately removed Franky's arm from around his neck.

"What gives?"

"He just had a fight," Val scolded Franky. "He's a little bent up."

Lay chuckled at Val's understanding. He nodded and felt his neck hurt just a little.

"Man, you did the damn thing," Franky said with a laugh and shake of his head.

Reg walked along with Lay. He did not reach out or say anything. He just shook his head in disbelief.

Darius too shook his head. Tamra was there as well and Lay could not connect the dots of why she, a Skittle, was with them. He studied Tamra and then Darius and then looked back at Val and Franky. No one offered an explanation. Lay wanted to know why Tamra, who had been riding with Cass and the Skittles crew, was suddenly with them, but at that moment he did not have the strength to ask.

They arrived at the front of old man Johnson's house. The steps were only a few feet away.

"Suppose we all need to touch the steps to seal the win," Val said.

Lay paused. He stretched his fingers and noticed his hand hurt. He walked up to the steps with Val and Franky and saw his right hand was a little swollen. There was blood on his scraped-up knuckles. He tried to close his hand and felt his hand refuse to close completely.

Like a walk off homerun all the Starburst crew touched the steps and laughed and talked as they took a much-needed moment to appreciate what Lay had accomplished.

Lay opened his mouth and felt a slight throb of pain in his jaw. He recalled that Cass had hit him there, but only now did he feel the effects. Lay tried to catalog all the places he felt pain.

His right hand felt like his hand was suffering from frostbite. It was tingling like there were ice crystals under his skin. Every time he tried to close his hand, he felt what seemed like thousands of jagged ice crystals rubbing underneath his knuckles.

"Does your hand hurt?"

Val was by him as they walked from old man Johnson's house to the sidewalk.

Lay did not speak. He didn't know what to say. He was not sure how to describe how his hand felt, exactly.

"I thought Cass was going to own Lay," Darius said.

"Do you remember that crazy move he put on Lay at the beginning of the fight," Reg said, imitating the leg kick Cass had done to pick up speed.

"Damn, you remember when Cass beat Lay in between the cars? I thought it was over then," Franky said.

Lay wondered if Cass had cut his head when he hit him? He did not feel any real pain in his head. His jaw hurt. His arms had been hit but they did not hurt any more than when he had been told by his uncle to do pushups.

He noticed his forearms were scratched but Lay could not recall how he had been scratched. He twisted his arm to see his left quadricep and noticed a cut there. He tried to recall how he had gotten cut there. He was beaten up, but not as badly as Cass or Ricky.

"I can't believe you mopped Cass," Franky said, with a shake of his head.

"I mean, I figured you were toast when he got the jump on you and beat you bad, at first," Reg said.

"I didn't think Lay was going to make it, but he did," Darius said with a laugh. "I mean, when you came back out onto the street. What were you thinking?"

"You know what he was thinking?" Franky said, with a laugh. "Don't let Cass hit me again."

"No, he was like, come on Cass, you think you so bad," Reg said, a big smile on his face.

"You know I think I need to start taking some self-defense lessons," Darius said, seriously. "Who taught you all that stuff?"

"It was really crazy stuff," Franky said. "I loved when stupid Ricky ran into Cass. You cannot make that stuff up."

"No, the best was when Lay hit Cass and froze Darryl," Reg said, with a laugh.

"No, the best was when Darryl stepped up," Darius said with a howl. "Lay just looked at him and Darryl froze."

"He was playing freeze tag by himself," Reg said with a cackle. Reg imitated Darryl standing but not moving.

Franky froze imitating Darryl.

"No, the best was Ricky," Darius said with a big smile on his face. He held his stomach and stuck out his hand like he was trying to touch the sky.

"You think they are coming back?"

"Don't think they are that stupid," Franky said. Franky looked at Reg and smiled. He hitched a thumb over his shoulder toward Lay who was standing on the sidewalk with Val next to him.

"Yeah, suppose you're right," Reg said, nodding. "He's like our very own bodyguard."

"He's our Drillbit Taylor," Franky said, with a smile.

"Naw, he's Ryan Reynolds in that movie with Samuel L. Jackson," Darius said. "The bodyguard's bodyguard. That guy was pretty cool."

Franky and Reg looked at Darius, curiously.

"How you get to see a Samuel L. Jackson movie?"

"My brother loves him and thinks I should watch all his movies, even the bad ones," Darius said.

"But he cusses a lot," Reg said.

"Yeah, my brother said we hear cussing all the time and it's our decision to use those words or not," Darius said, with a shrug of his shoulders.

Val was near Lay as he stood on the sidewalk looking across the street where he had to go next.

"What are you thinking about?"

Lay gave Val a side glance. He remembered what she said the first time he and Cass fought. Now, that Lay had won Val was suddenly all concerned about him. He wanted to smile at the idea.

"Nothing," Lay said feeling his jaw fight against his muscles. He was lying.

Lay was thinking that just a few minutes ago he had faced down three of the Skittles crew and nearly been stabbed with a knife. He had done what his uncle had taught him, and he had practiced and shut down the two biggest bullies on the block and shamed the third.

According to his uncle those three were not going to be an issue in the future. If anyone was spoiling for a fight it would be someone new who had missed out on Lay's fight. The eleven-year-old closed his eyes to the future on Twentieth Street.

All he cared about that moment was that Twentieth Street was once again quiet. Cass and Ricky were gone. They had been picked up and hauled away by their friends. In their absence the stars above seemed a little brighter.

Now, as Lay stood the soreness of the fight slowly began to wash over him. He needed to sit down and rest for a day or two. He was cut and bleeding. He was bruised and just wanted to sit down, but the night wasn't over.

"You ready for this?"

Lay looked at Val and nodded. Lay moved stiffly trying to relax and let his muscles relax, but his hand throbbed like there were tiny bees beneath his skin stinging him every time he moved.

"We have to get our stuff," Franky said.

Lay stood and looked at the four-foot fence that bordered the Stewart sister's house.

The Starburst crew crossed the street and all the conversation quieted as they stepped on the opposite curb and moved to the sidewalk.

Chapter 22. Stewart Sisters

The red brick house sat back some thirty feet from the sidewalk. It was guarded by a four-foot chain-link gate that anyone could jump over. Yet, on either side of the low gate and all the way to the alley stretched a ten-foot high and trimmed hedge of some of the toughest waxy leaves imaginable. The front yard had six trees planted in its spacious front. The tallest tree was near the porch. The other five trees sat throughout the property.

From the sidewalk the house was barely visible in the shadows cast by the hedge and trees. At night, the house became almost impossible to see unless there was a light on to guide anyone to the front door.

The house was not gigantic but modest and sat on a spacious bit of green, just three houses from Randolph Street. The lawn and hedges were always manicured and immaculate.

Randolph Street was the bottom of the street where the Becks lived. At the other end of the block was Oak Street. Oak Street was the street Hanna, Jordan and Lay walked on everyday afterschool. Randolph Street was also the usual border of the play where Lay and the others stopped. For Lay, he looked past Randolph Street and toward Washington Boulevard and the block where Penny lived. Lay only stepped crossed Randolph Street with Jay.

Now, barring the creepiness of the Stewart house and the hedges and the shadowy nature of the house and it being set back from the sidewalk, most did not dare to play near the house because of Queenie, Dutchess and Nessa.

In the rear of the Stewart yard was a taller chain-link fence which delineated the backyard from the front and where the three beasts resided. The three beasts were gigantic creatures that were wild-eyed and continually barking and threatening to jump over the fence and eat anyone foolish enough to trespass on the Stewart property.

"I hate coming over here," Val said to Lay who was sucking on his lower lip to stop the bleeding.

"Well, who's going to go up there and get our stuff?" Frank asked, sheepishly.

The Starburst crew looked at each other uncertain.

Luckily, Zeke reappeared with a few spots of blood on the shoulders of his T-shirt, after the fight was over and the Skittles crew dispersed.

"What happened to you?" Reg pointed to the blood on Zeke's shirt.

Zeke looked at the blood and back at Reg and the Starburst crew.

"That's Huey's blood, not mine."

"How's Huey?" Darius asked.

"Is he okay?" Frank asked, concerned.

"He has some cuts and scrapes and they stomped him out pretty good," Zeke said as the Starburst group stood in front of the Stewart sister's house.

"He, okay?"

"Was Huey ever really, okay?" Zeke asked.

"Yeah, you got a point," Val said with a smile.

"What did you tell his mother?"

"I told her he fell down in the alley and cut himself," Zeke said to Reg. "It's basically true."

The six stood on the sidewalk in front of the Stewart sister's house.

"Okay, go get our goods," Darius said.

"Anybody want to go with me?"

"You should take Lay, he ain't afraid of those spooky sisters," Val said, pushing Lay forward.

Lay, who was nursing his busted lip shrugged his shoulders and followed Zeke up the walkway to the darkened porch. Val, at the last minute, followed along. Darius, Reg and Franky reluctantly followed.

As the Starburst crew approached the house the dogs began to bark.

"Shut up," said Page in the darkness of the porch. Her voice was gravelly. She had one of those heavy voices like an old woman that smoked every day.

Darius, Reg and Franky bumped into each other trying to return to the sidewalk. Reg broke through the two others and Franky followed. The last to make it back to the sidewalk was Darius.

"Queenie, shut up," Regine said as well, and the dogs quieted.

Zeke, Val and Lay climbed onto the porch. The sisters were sitting in dark chairs on the dark porch.

"You know you didn't tell us that these cards had a value on 'em," Page said.

"Yeah, I did a Google search and found that one of these books is worth more than five dollars," Regine said, giving Lay and Val the side eye.

Val narrowed her dark eyes. She balled her fists ready to fight.

Lay looked at Val and smiled. He reached out and held Val back.

"This box of Negro League baseball cards is pretty pricey," Page said with a mirthless smile.   "Where did you get 'em?"

"That's none of your business," Val said through clenched teeth.

"Think we got shortchanged on this deal," Regine said in the darkness.

"The price is the price," Zeke said calmly.

"Think we need to renegotiate the price," Regine said.

"Why?"

"Because it is worth more than five dollars," Page said in her raspy voice.

"You mean, if it was a rock, you wouldn't care that you agreed to five dollars?"

"Well, yeah," Regine said.

"Okay, so how did you figure out that they were comics and baseball cards?"

"Well, we looked," Page said in her husky tone.

"That wasn't part of the deal," Zeke pointed out.

"But," Page said, in the shadows of the porch.

"But you told us that for five dollars you would make sure no one messed with our stuff and it would be safe. You remember that?" Zeke said. "That included you."

Regine twisted her lips on her dark brown face.

Page smiled.

Regine handed Zeke his backpack.

Page looked at Regine.

"Sometime all we got is our reputation," Regine said dryly.

Page reluctantly handed Lay the other backpack with the baseball cards.

Val and Lay turned to leave.

"Hey, Lay," Regine said in the darkness.

Lay turned around with the Skittles backpack over his shoulder.

"Good job, tonight," Page said, her voice raspy.

Lay nodded.

"You don't talk much," Regine said from the darkness.

Lay turned and he and Val walked down the steps of the darkened porch. Zeke followed behind.

At the bottom of the steps the three dogs started barking again.

"Queenie, shut up," one of the sisters said.

Lay, carrying the Skittles backpack followed Val to the sidewalk where Darius, Franky and Reg were waiting. Zeke joined them a few seconds later.

"What do we do now?"

"Well, the first thing is give me back my comics," Val said.

"Then we divide the spoils," Reg said with a big smile on his oval face.

"Where do you want to go?"

"We can go to my house it's on the other side of old man Johnson's house," Val admitted.

No one objected and Val lead the way to her house. She was two houses up from the Stewart's house on the opposite side of the street. The boys carrying the backpacks were surrounded by Darius and Tamra and Franky and Reg.

"I got dibs on that Ken Griffey Rookie card," Franky said as they walked toward Val's house.

"I want that box set of Blasters," Darius said, looking at Franky.

"I think I want that Negro League box set," said Reg.

Then they were at Val's house. The porch was not the typical porch. There were a dozen stairs that led to the front door. At the top of the stairs was a small landing where half a dozen people could stand comfortably. Val walked to the top of the stairs and sat down. Darius and Tamra sat on the steps one step below the landing Franky and Reg climbed up the steps and sat on the landing. Lay climbed the steps with Zeke and when Zeke got to the landing, he shucked the backpack and sat on the landing.

"Think I'm going," said Tamra, climbing to her feet.

Everyone looked at Tamra and Darius. Darius awkwardly looked at his friends and then Tamra. He climbed to his feet and walked to the bottom of the steps with Tamra.

At the bottom of the stairs Tamra and Darius talked briefly and Darius reached out for a hug. Tamra pushed him away with her arms. She turned and walked to her bike. She climbed on her mountain bike and rode up the street toward Oak Street.

"Okay, someone clue me in," said Lay, confused.

Darius walked back up the steps and everyone was looking at him with amused looks on their faces. Lay was the only one who seemed out of the loop.

"Darius got a girlfriend," said Reg with a chuckle.

Everyone laughed. Val shook her head. Darius too shook his head.

"When did that happen?"

"Don't worry about it," said Val to Lay, bored by the whole situation.

"Good job, son," Zeke said to Darius like a proud papa.

"Shut up," Darius said, annoyed. "It ain't like that."

"What's it like?"

Darius shot Franky a cold stare.

"Don't get all sensitive on me, lover boy," Franky said.

"Hey, I thought we came here to get our stuff back," Val said, annoyed.

Zeke opened the backpack and returned all the comic books to their rightful owners. There was one comic book left in the backpack. Zeke pulled out the black and white comic book cover with a scribble across the corner of the right edge of the book. It was cardboard backed and sealed in plastic.

"Who's going to take that to Huey?"

No one moved.

"I can't go again," Zeke said. "I mean, I just dropped him off and I cannot go back and knock on the door and say: Hey, Miss Cooper, Huey dropped this in the alley. I just wanted to return it."

"Why not?" Asked Reg.

"Yeah, that sounds reasonable," said Franky, with a grin. Franky still had Huey's shoes on his shoulder.

"I'll take it," said Val. She reached out and grabbed the pair of gym shoes on Franky's shoulder.

Lay slid the Skittles backpack toward Zeke.

"You guys figure that out," Lay said climbing to his feet. "I think I'm going to get grilled by my fam," he said, looking across the street and seeing three dark shadows on the porch just one hundred yards away.

"Good luck," Val said and touched Lay gently on the arm. Lay looked at Val curiously and looked back across the street. Zeke, Franky, Reg and Darius patted Lay on the shoulder as he walked down the steps and to the sidewalk.

Lay paused on the sidewalk and looked at Twentieth Street in the dark. The streetlights. The parked cars. He looked down the street and back the other way before crossing and making his way to the Beck's house.

Chapter 23. Family Matters

Having just dealt with the excitement and happiness of the Starburst crew Lay crossed the street slowly. He tried to imagine what he was going to walk into when he stepped in his cousin's house. A dozen steps propelled him from one side of the street to the other and he looked back. His friends were heading home.

Darius, Reg and Franky were walking up the street toward their homes. Zeke who lived on the corner was turning into his front yard. Reg cut across the street a few houses above the Victorian apartment house and disappeared into the dark. Val climbed up the front stairs of her house holding Huey's sneakers by the knotted laces in between her thumb and forefinger like they were two dead rats. She deposited the sneakers on the porch and walked into her home.

Lay dreaded what was coming from his cousins. He knew they had seen him fighting. All of Twentieth Street had to see the fight. It was in the middle of the street. Lay thought, for a moment, before he walked up onto the porch, what he was going to say.

"I had no choice," Lay imagined would be a good deflection. "I mean, did you want me to be knifed in the street? Did you want me dead?"

He knew if he made it past Hanna or his aunt the one woman who would not listen to anything he said was his mother.

"Lay, I sent you to your cousins to keep you out of trouble," she would begin. She would break down in tears and tell Lay how he didn't love her. "If you loved me, you wouldn't make me worry."

There was no way to win with his mother.

Luckily, Lay did not have to deal with his mother then and there. Instead, he had his cousins and aunt and uncle to contend with. Compared to his mother they were pushovers.

He walked up the walkway to the porch of the Beck's house and slowly, reluctantly climbed up the steps to the porch with his Batman comic book in his left hand. At the top of the steps the porch light snapped on. When the light popped on, he was sure he heard the titter of laughter behind the front door.

Lay stopped and waited. He knew his cousins were on the other side of the door. He just didn't know if they were going to wait for him to reach the door before they opened it and rushed him.

On the porch, under the porch light, Lay watched as moths appeared from the darkness to circle the light. The eleven-year-old stood and listened to the quiet of Twentieth Street. Everyone was on their way home. Lay was going to open the screen door and deal with his cousins and their questions.

Maybe, Lay thought, he would ask Hanna to patch him up like she had when Cass cut him above his left eye. Then and there all he wanted was to close his eyes and sleep for a few hours. Yet, he knew sleep was not going to be immediate.

The eleven-year-old took a deep breath and crossed to the screen door. He depressed the latch and pulled on the door and there on the other side was Jordan smiling from ear-to-ear like he had won a prize.

Behind him was Hanna smiling big and broad her hands on her hips. Beside Hanna was Jay. Jay was smiling one of those big smiles you see on the Colgate commercials.

"Well, if it ain't the Cass Crusher," said Jordan with a toothy grin. Jordan threw a few punches and Hanna reached out and put her hands on her younger brother's shoulders to stop his animated fighting.

"Lathan Alexander I was impressed," Hanna said gushing, her round cheeks swelling. She tilted her head and smiled at Lay.

"Good job, little man," Jay said with a grin.

Lay laughed at the kind words from Jordan and Hanna. Behind the two Jay nodded and beckoned Lay to come inside.

Lay stepped gingerly inside the Beck house and instantly Jordan and Hanna were hugging him, despite his protests. Lay pushed them away.

"You, okay?" Jay asked, concerned.

Lay shook his head. He showed Hanna his hand, the scratches and the back of his arm.

"That's just a scratch," Hanna said releasing his arm.

Lay listened and looked behind his cousins to his aunt who was standing near the dining room with a big smile on her face, her arms crossed in front of her.

"Mama," Hanna said grabbing Lay by the shoulder and leading him deeper into the house.

"Jay, can you take care of my comic?"

"Yeah, sure," Jay said with a smile as Hanna took Lay to her mother.

Aunt Bree, still smiling, looked at Lay.

"I saw you out there," Aunt Bree said.

Lay looked down at his shoe tops.

"You ain't got nothing to be ashamed of Lay," she said checked Lay's injuries. "That little boy has been terrorizing the neighborhood for a while."

Lay looked up at his aunt's big eyes behind her glasses. Hanna had her mother's eyes and round cheeks. Aunt Bree smiled and patted Lay on the cheek. She examined Lay's injuries. The worse was his swollen hand.

"Can you squeeze your hand?"

Lay tried but it felt like his fingers were sausages instead of fingers.

"Does it hurt?"

Lay shook his head, no.

"Well, it's not broke," Aunt Bree said. "Jordan go to the refrigerator and get me a bag of frozen peas, baby."

Jordan disappeared.

"Hanna, clean him up," Aunt Bree said. "You'll be fine. Just scrapes and bruises. I've seen worse." His aunt smiled and patted Lay on the cheek. "You probably need to just rest."

Jordan returned with the frozen peas. He gave it to his mother. Aunt Bree placed it on Lay's right hand.

"Keep that on there for twenty minutes," Aunt Bree said. "It will help the swelling go down."

"That's it?" Lay asked, concerned about his hand.

"You hit someone with your hand, Lay," Aunt Bree said with a slight grin. "What did you expect? From what I saw you didn't just hit someone once but a few times. Your hand is made of flesh and bone. It hurt them. Now, it hurts. It, you, will be fine."

Lay nodded.

Jay was suddenly beside Lay as Hanna marched Lay to the small bathroom.

"Put that on your knuckles," Jay said to Lay. "Good you didn't break anything."

"He should have broke Cass's nose," Jordan said, trying to squeeze into the small bathroom.

Hanna cleaned Lay's cuts and scratches and bandaged the long three-inch scratch on the back of his arm with ointment and gauze.

"What was the scariest part," Jordan asked from the doorway of the bathroom.

"The knife," Lay said to his younger cousin.

"That punk is really dangerous," Hanna said checking Lay's busted lip. She shook her head. "You're going to be sore for a couple of days, but at eleven you are still kind of rubbery. You'll be fine."

Hanna threw away the trash and Lay walked out of the bathroom to Jay.

Lay stopped and looked at Hanna who was smiling at her younger cousin.

Jay reached out and put a hand on Lay's shoulder.

Jordan was all smiles.

Hanna stepped out the bathroom and smiled.

"What's going on?"

Lay reached out and hugged his older cousins and Jordan.

"What's all this?"

"Group hug," said Jordan, reaching out and hugging his brother and sister and Lay.

"Hey, Lathan Alexander, what are you doing?"

"Just love you all," Lay said. "Thank you." He loved the love of his cousins. He loved being with the Becks. He loved being on Twentieth the summer he learned to play Monopoly and Chase.

Pulling back the curtain

When I began writing <u>The Chase</u>, I initially thought the story would be more interesting if Lay had to walk to his cousins on Twentieth from November until school let out in May. For a lot of reasons, it made sense, but it became kind of long and parts of it just dragged. I struggled with the timeframe. I knew I wanted the story to pivot around the whole idea of Lay and his friends preparing for the end of their youthful childhood summer and the inevitable move away from childish things, but I wanted a buildup to that moment. I like to write the idea out in outline format and as I looked over the story arc, I realized there was no place for the winter part of the story. If you recall one of the characters notes the same thing. It is me talking to me about letting go of this concept.

Here are two chapters which did not make it to the final edition. If you like Lay, you might like him trapped on Twentieth during the winter by himself in the Beck house with measles. Again, in the original, longer form, Lay and his mother visit the Becks for Christmas and then there is the eventual push to the end of school.

I liked these chapters. They were fresh and unsullied by the limitations of the story. They were crafted to show another side of Lay. These two chapters show a side of Lay that is alluded to in the overall story. They were good but honestly, I could not figure out a way to include them in this book. So, I threw them in here to show how I struggled with letting go of Lay, even as I finished. I really like Lathan Payton Alexander.

I love his struggle. Writing is very personal no matter what people tell you. The ideas, characters, settings, rest upon me and when I write I often stop to listen to the characters talking. I love Lay and Underwood and all the craziness despite the story morphing and moving in another direction.

Chapter 24. Measles

For most of the school year, rain or shine, snow or flurries, Lay, at the end of the school day, met up with Hanna and Jordan at the rear of the school and along with all the others walked from the eastside of the Underwood to the westside of the Underwood. Lay noted the school year in his clothing. At the beginning of the walks to the westside of the Underwood most kids were in short sleeves, jeans and sneakers. When it rained, before winter arrived, most walking ahead of him were in raincoats, the older girls carried umbrellas, and Lay just wore a plastic poncho over his school clothes and sneakers. He always forgot to wear his rubber boots.

Lay wished his mother would have changed her mind about his staying over Hanna's when the snow fell. The walk from school to Twentieth was a cold and bitter march sometimes against the biting wind and falling snow. On the walk, Lay would catch some of the smaller kids caught up in the wonder and quiet of the winter. It was as if they were not walking down streets, they walked down every day but in their very own snow globes and inside the sound of the world was unexplainably unable to penetrate.

In the bone chilling cold Lay found the silence and snow-covered things he took for granted transformed into marvelous snow sculptures. Trees were no longer trees but the endless beginnings of snow arches he and the other kids ran in and out of just because. Cars covered with snow became giant snow turtles sleeping at the snow arches.

Over Christmas break Jordan got sick and that meant everyone got sick in the Beck household. It was just inevitable. Jordan was always hugging on everyone even when they protested.

So, when Hanna became the second to succumb to the unknown sickness everyone expected either Lay or Jay to be next. Hanna bet on Lay. Jordan laid in bed aching and weak.

The third person in the Beck family to fall to the Jordan sickness was Jay. When Jay got sick his mother took him to the hospital, and they determined Jay had the measles.

Everyone expected Lay to fall ill as well but for three days he soldiered on and then one morning he woke up on Sixth Street with a stomachache. Before he could eat breakfast, he vomited. He lay in bed the entire day, and when his mother found him in bed, she knew he was sick.

"Am I dying?"

"No, silly, you are sick," his mother said.

"What is it?"

"I think you have the measles," his mother said, picking up the phone and calling her brother and sister-in-law.

"What are we going to do?"

"Let me worry about that," his mother said.

She bundled up Lay and drove him to Twentieth where Jordan, Jay and Hanna were still in the grips of the recently diagnosed sickness. They were shells of themselves, Lay noted as his aunt smiled and ushered Lay into her house. His mother waved goodbye from the car and drove off to work.

"How come my mom didn't come in?"

"Well, we've all had measles, but we can never be too careful," his aunt said.

Lay had no energy to argue. His mind was foggy. His body hurt. He was incredibly tired. All he wanted to do was lay down. Well, he wanted to have a cup of water and lay down.

A week went by and Jordan seemed to regain his strength. Ten days after Lay arrived in the makeshift hospital Jordan was his annoying self. He sat up and watched TV and ate and drank and suddenly was cleared to return to school. Jay was the second to be released. Hanna, the ever watchful, was the last of the Beck trio to return to school and the first to relieve her mother in the makeshift hospital on Twentieth.

Five days after Hanna was back in school Lay found himself feeling his strength return. He recalled he had celebrated his twelfth birthday in the empty house on Twentieth. His aunt had gone out to get groceries while he was asleep, and Lay had woken to find himself alone and twelve. He wrapped the covers around his still feverish body and walked to the front window to see the white clad streets, houses, cars and trees. If he did not know better Lay might have thought himself dreaming. Out of the window, he could see the plowed streets and the shoveled walkways, but it was the green wood porch which reminded the newly minted twelve-year old he was not dreaming.

When his aunt returned home, she found Lay sitting in the living room on the couch.

"You feeling better?"

Lay nodded.

"I can tell," his aunt said and smiled. "These measles are tough on the body. Seems like you should be up and right as rain maybe tomorrow or the next day," his aunt said. She was a short and compact woman with full lips, round cheeks, shoulder length hair and small eyes behind rimless glasses. She reminded Lay of a female teddy bear.

Aunt Bree's words rang in his ears a few days later when Lay began to feel better. He had gotten over measles. He returned to school the next week.

Chapter 25. Missus Truitt

When Lay returned to school after overcoming his measles no one said anything about his absence. He had work to turn in. He had done all the work while laid up at his cousin's house. His teachers smiled a lot finding Lay had returned but they did not say anything about his absence. It was a strange return.

Lay tried to think why no one welcomed him back. He looked around his classroom and understood that he, in the three years at Saint Paul Catholic School, had not made any real friends. His teachers who never had a bad word about him did not even have a good word to say about Lay's return.

The thing about no acknowledgement of his return spoke volumes to Lay. He sat in the classrooms and tried to figure out what he had done to not merit any attention while gone, or more importantly, when he returned.

At lunch Lay went to talk to one of his teachers.

"Missus Truitt, can I talk to you?"

"Sure, Lay, what is it?"

"Well, I was wondering if you think I'm a good person," Lay said looking at the white woman with the big, puffy blonde hair, a choker chain of pearls, a white blouse and manicured nails sitting behind her desk. She had a flat face, arched eyebrows above her blue eyes and thin nose and lips.

Missus Truitt smiled on the other side of the desk. She had her lunch of a diet soda, an orange and a sandwich on her desk. The sandwich was still in a plastic zip top bag. She tilted her diamond shaped head to the left and then the right, puckering her thin lips as she looked at Lay.

"Well, I would say you are a good student, Lay," Missus Truitt said.

Lay nodded. "Well, you know I was out of school for nearly three weeks," Lay said. "Did you notice?"

"Of course," Missus Truitt said. "We were told you had the measles. I had the class send you a Get Well Soon card." She paused. "You didn't get the card?"

"Who would have given it to me?"

"Well, we sent it to the office. They probably mailed it to your home," Missus Truitt said.

Lay nodded. "Thanks," Lay said as he walked away from his teacher.

Hanna and Jordan watched over Lay the first week he returned to school on the walk to Twentieth.

"You doing okay?" Jordan asked, suddenly beside Lay.

"Yeah, I'm fine," Lay said.

Jordan nodded and returned to annoying everyone on the walk.

Hanna made sure that Lay and Jordan were near her when she crossed the avenue. Lay did not complain. He didn't know how to complain at the unusual attention from his cousins.

The Monday Lay returned to school and walked to his cousin's house he was preoccupied. He could not understand why his mother had not told him the school had sent him a letter. Almost immediately, Lay flipped his thoughts on their head. Why would his mother not tell him? The idea of his mother not telling him something like that seemed impossible. What made more sense was that Missus Truitt was lying. Maybe, Lay thought, as he waited for his mother to pick him up, Missus Truitt had made up the story to make Lay feel better. She did not think Lay would check. If Lay went home and found no letter, Missus Truitt would say, it was lost in the mail. It was an easy excuse.

The horn beeped outside and Lay gathered his things and told his cousins and aunt goodbye. He left and climbed into the Volkswagen and smiled at his mother behind the wheel ready to drive them home.

The envelope from the Saint Paul Catholic School was sitting on the kitchen table when they returned home. Lay wanted to scream when he saw it. He wanted to snatch it up and run around the apartment. Seeing the envelope verified what Missus Truitt had told him.

"Ma, how come you didn't tell me that the school sent me a letter?"

"What? I don't know, I didn't think it was that important," his mother said. "I had more important things to worry about."

"But, Ma," Lay began.

"Lay, I'm tired, I just need to rest. I don't want to go back and forth with you over a letter. You got a letter. Your school sent you a letter.

Are you happy? Is that what you wanted me to say? I said it," his mother said and picked up the phone and dialed a number. She opened the refrigerator and pulled out some cold leftovers and began to make something for the pair to eat.

Lay could not argue with his mother even when he thought she missed the point. He had received a Get Well Soon card from his classmates. They had taken the time to write to him personally and wish him good health.

After dinner Lay picked up the Saint Paul Catholic School letter and walked to his bedroom. In the quiet of his bedroom, he opened the letter carefully. It was the first letter addressed to him. Inside the envelope was a Get Well Soon card. On the cover the card read: Sending You Big Hugs and Get Well Wishes. Lay smiled at the cover. It was a store-bought card. He opened the card and read all the well wishes. There were a bunch of scribbled names he could not make out. Missus Truitt's cursive signature was in the middle of the other scrawls.

The next day Lay thanked everyone for the Get Well Soon card. For all the lack of acknowledgement of his absence the realization his classmates had taken the time to sign a card wishing him a fast recovery from the measles was as uncomfortable as not being seen or considered to Lay. He was not sure he wanted his classmates to care about him. Yet, simultaneously, he did not want to be unseen and invisible.